TOM HALL

and the Captain of All
These Men of Death

TOM HALL

and the Captain of All These Men of Death

A NOVEL BY RUSSELL HILL

Pleasure Boat Studio: A Literary Press
New York

Tom Hall
by Russell Hill

ISBN 978-0-912887-25-8
Library of Congress Control Number: TBA

Cover by Laura Tolkow
Design by Susan Ramundo

Pleasure Boat Studio books are available through the following:
SPD (Small Press Distribution) Tel. 800-869-7553, Fax 510-524-0852
Partners/West Tel. 425-227-8486, Fax 425-204-2448
Baker & Taylor Tel. 800-775-1100, Fax 800-775-7480
Ingram Tel. 615-793-5000, Fax 615-287-5429
Amazon.com and **bn.com**

and through
PLEASURE BOAT STUDIO: A LITERARY PRESS
www.pleasureboatstudio.com
201 West 89th Street
New York, NY 10024

Contact **Jack Estes**
Fax: 413-677-0085
Email: pleasboat@nyc.rr.com

"The captain of all these men of death that came against him to take him away, was the Consumption for it was that that brought him down to the grave."

The Life and Death of Mr. Badman
John Bunyan, 1680

PROLOGUE

I came back to Kentucky when my mother died. I had not lived there in years, only the occasional visit when business took me as far east as Chicago or St. Louis. When my sister phoned and I heard her soft Kentucky drawl, I knew something was wrong.

"Mother died," was all she said.

"When?" I asked.

"Last night. You'll be here tomorrow."

It wasn't a command. Just a statement of fact in the way my sister had of stripping her voice of all pretence. No show about her. Her speech was as plain as the clothes she wore and the three children she had raised and the husband who worked the small Kentucky farm and watched TV from his Barcalounger after dinner and drove them all to the State Fair once a year where her children showed their 4-H lambs. It was hard to believe that my mother was her mother, too.

So I boarded a plane and flew to Lexington and rented a car and drove south through Lancaster into Lincoln County, and then on the two-lane blacktop through a series of tiny towns whose names were familiar although I had not been through any of them in ten years: Crab Orchard, Dogwalk, Bandy, Woodstock, until I reached Dabney. Although the drive took less than two hours, it seemed as if I had traveled for days.

My sister had made all the arrangements, including a simple wooden casket.

"No point in wasting a lot of money on something that's just going to rot in the ground," she said.

My mother, who had lived the last few years in a room in my sister's house, had left very little. Pamela had already given her clothes to the church, and had cleaned out the room by the time I arrived.

"You can sleep here," she said. It had not occurred to her, I suppose, that I might feel strange sleeping in the bed in which my mother had died only a few nights before, but the room was empty, there were clean sheets, and as far as she was concerned, staying in a motel would be foolish.

"People would think we don't get along," she said, ignoring the fact that we hadn't had much contact over the past twenty years. At eighteen I had left Dabney to go north to Ohio State University and hadn't looked back. My freshman year I consciously scrubbed the Kentucky out of my voice.

After the funeral we sat in the kitchen while people I didn't know came by, greeted me as if they knew me, talked, and left food until finally, jet-lagged and exhausted, I went to bed. But I couldn't sleep.

My mother had been buried in the family plot, and there, at the head of the hole where they had lowered the coffin, was the headstone with my father's name, Edward Hall, and the years inscribed, 1913–1946. And now, in the small room where she had died, a few of her things that my sister supposed I might want were neatly arranged on a small table: a photograph of me and my father on the Boardwalk in Santa Monica; my school report cards that mother had saved; a copy of the 1954 Ohio State literary magazine with my first published short story; and the thin leather money belt that Larry had bought for me to wear underneath my trousers that spring when I had come to Kentucky for the first time. As I fingered the belt I thought about the long train ride east and about the other train ride west that my father that I had made and the eight months when I had lived on the far side of the moon.

ARIZONA

1

IT WAS MID-AFTERNOON when the train stopped. There was a general jerking and screeching of brakes and then silence. I was hot and tired. My father and I had been on the train for two and a half days, sleeping in the chair car, gradually feeling dirtier and sweatier as the train had come farther west.

Now the train was stopped and my father struggled to get our suitcase down from the overhead rack. He was a slightly built man and in his weakened condition it looked as if the scuffed leather bag would come crashing down on him.

I was twelve. The year was 1945.

We had come to Arizona because my father had tuberculosis. In those days you went west, to places like Arizona or New Mexico, preferably up in the mountains where the thin dry air was supposed to help cure the disease. I don't know how my father found the place. I suppose a doctor told him about it. Apparently there were dozens of sanatoriums, or "sans" as they called them, filled with men and women who left the cold damp winters of the northeast and midwest to air out their lungs in the arid mountains of the southwest.

We left the South Side of Chicago, the two of us, one suitcase between us, on the Santa Fe Railroad at the end of the summer. My mother had disappeared at the end of July. My father, who had been working at Arlington Park racetrack as a teller had been getting steadily thinner and weaker and he had been coughing more and more. At first we thought it was a bad winter cold, but when it lasted into the summer and it got deeper and deeper until he was racked by paroxysms of coughing, bent double, and it seemed he would cough up his lungs, we knew it was more than a cold that wouldn't go away. In June he went to see a doctor and the doctor diagnosed tuberculosis. My mother, who was never very good around sick people anyway, began to talk about going home to Kentucky, and in the middle of July she simply left. No note, no goodbye. Just packed her clothes, emptied out what little there was in the bank account, and left. She took my sister, Pamela, who was eight, with her. Looking back on it I suppose it was her way of dividing things up. She got the money and Pamela, my father got the furniture, such as it was, and me. The house was rented, so there was nothing else left. But there was more to it than that and I would not figure it out until the year was nearly over.

My father told me about the tuberculosis, but he told me not to tell anyone else and he continued to go to the racetrack each day. I wasn't sure what tuberculosis was, but I watched my father get weaker and weaker until the end of summer when he came home one evening and announced we were going to Arizona.

It was mid-afternoon when the train stopped in Williams. Actually, it didn't stop in Williams, it stopped twenty miles west of Williams at a place called Navajo Junction. I was excited because Navajo meant Indians, and I fully expected to see them, astride their spotted ponies, perhaps not in full battle dress as I'd seen them pictured in my eighth-grade history book, but still looking very Indian-like, and I was disappointed to find that Navajo Junction wasn't anything more than a place where a graveled road crossed the railroad tracks. There was a wooden building next to the tracks that looked as if it might have been a station at one time, but the roof had worn away in places, and the boards were curling and unpainted. The remains of a platform sloped away from one side of the building. Other than that, there was nothing there.

We stood in the gravel as the conductor put the metal footstool in the vestibule, climbed up on the lower step, leaned out, and waved. There was a jerk and a rumble and the train started moving.

A minute later it was growing smaller down the tracks and my father and I were alone.

"Shit!" I heard my father mutter. Which was surprising, because my father never swore. At least I had never heard him swear. We sat in the shade of the abandoned station, our backs against the weathered wall, looking at the mountains in the distance, blue-gray in the afternoon heat. We must have sat there silently for half an hour before a plume of dust appeared several miles off. As it approached, I could see that it was being made by a vehicle, and it wasn't long after that a beat-up Ford panel truck came down the gravel road toward us. The driver waved one hand out the window as if to announce his arrival, but it was obvious that his was the only vehicle coming and we were the only people waiting.

The truck came to a stop with a flourish, turning broadside to the road, and the driver leaped out, going around to the back and opening the two doors. Inside were four kitchen chairs bolted to the walls of the truck, two on either side. The man, a short fellow with a smile that seemed to split his brown face horizontally, didn't say anything, just grabbed our bag and tossed it in between the chairs on the dusty floor of the truck.

"Are you from Metzenbaum's Sanatorium?" my father asked.

"*Si*," the man replied.

"I'm Edward Hall and this is my son, Thomas," my father said, but the man interrupted him with a wave of his hand, shaking it back and forth in front of my father's face.

"*No habla Inglés*," the man said.

"No what?" My father asked.

"*No habla Inglés, No Eenglis.*" He waved us toward the inside of the truck.

"Jesus Christ," my father muttered, climbing over the rear bumper. The man shut the doors behind us and we sat in the semi-darkness, the only light coming from the windshield, visible over the back of the driver's seat.

"Where are we going?" I asked.

"To Doctor Metzenbaum's tuberculosis sanatorium," my father replied. He reached out and touched my shoulder. My father was not a toucher, so the gesture took on added significance.

"It's not exactly what I was told," he said. "But maybe it's just a different way of life out West."

The West. The very words excited me.

2

IN ONE OF THE GALLERIES in the art museum in Chicago hung a painting that I always sought out when we were there. It showed two Indians on their horses, looking out over a long valley. One of them was wrapped in a striped blanket, the other had his arm extended, as if he were pointing out some far distant object. The foreground was rocky and dotted with sagebrush, but the long stretch of landscape beyond them was almost purple, white-topped mountains rising out of the hazy distance, gray clouds scudding across the sky. When I woke up at Metzenbaum's sanatorium that first morning and went out onto the lawn in front of the building where I had slept, I found that only the Indians were missing. Even though I had watched great distances unfold from the train during the past three days, the plains dropping away from Metzenbaum's mountainside sanatorium were hard to grasp. In Chicago there had always been buildings, and even the horizon of Lake Michigan hadn't been like this, because I could turn right or left and see the city blocking the sky.

Somewhere in front of me the Grand Canyon cut its swath through the earth, to the right were mountains cloaked in dense pines, and far off to the left the dim outlines of the mountains of New Mexico rose in the early morning light. It was as if I had stepped through the screen during the Saturday morning movie on the South Side of Chicago and found myself waiting for Zachary Scott and a troop of cavalry soldiers to appear. I immediately set off to find where my father had spent the night so I could share my excitement with him.

The patients were housed in small square cottages, each with four beds, one against each wall. There were windows along each side, almost the whole length of the cottage, only there was no glass, only screens. Outside, a solid shutter was hinged at the top, and they were all propped open by long poles that were wedged at the base of the building. In the winter these shutters could be lowered to enclose the cottage, but all summer they were raised, giving each little house the appearance of a Chinese coolie's hat. You could stand at one side of the building and look right through, in one window and out the windows on the opposite side.

The floors were wooden, polished over and over until they had a dull shine, worn pale at the edge of each bed and the doorway.

Each man had a dresser at the foot of his bed, a night stand with a lamp at the head of the bed, and in the middle of the room was a small square wood stove with a stovepipe that rose straight through the roof. The rafters of the building were exposed, and it had a camp-like feeling, as if these men had come to the mountains for the summer and would go swimming and make lanyards and sing songs around the campfire and then, when the nights got cold, would get on the bus and go back to the cities they had come from.

My father's bed was the one on the wall with the doorway. Because of the door he had less room than the others, but it was expected that the newcomer in the cottage would get the short wall. The beds were high and made of iron with enough room underneath for boxes where the men kept personal belongings other than clothing. When I climbed up on my father's bed I discovered that it was level with the low window sill. I could lie on the bed and look to my left and see the Sangre de Cristo Mountains stretching beyond the piñon trees, green at first, fading into a hazy blue.

But I would learn that I wasn't supposed to lie on his bed. In fact, I wasn't supposed to hang around the cottage at all. I would be given a room in the nurse's wing of the main hospital, a low-slung building with wide overhanging eaves. Hospital was a generous term. It was more like a big family home, with a room for an x-ray machine, an examining room, Dr. Metzenbaum's office, a big kitchen at one end where they prepared the meals for the san, a dining room, a couple of private rooms for patients who were seriously ill, and a lounge for the nurses. Only one of the nurses stayed at the san. The other two lived in Vallecitos, a few miles down the mountain. My room wasn't much bigger than a closet, room enough for a bed and a small dresser. It had a single high window I could only see the sky through, and I spent very little time in it. The whole sanatorium consisted of six cottages, the hospital, and a little house where Dr. Metzenbaum lived, all connected by graveled paths that wound among tall pines.

The first morning I watched my father arrange his things on the table next to his bed and stow the suitcase under it, and he introduced me to the three other men.

"You'll have to entertain yourself for a while, Tommy," he said. "I'm afraid there may not be other kids around,"

"That's okay," I said. I was used to moving, and making new friends wasn't something I set high on my list. Racetrack meetings ended and we'd pack our things and friends disappeared with a dependable regularity.

A large man in a white smock opened the screen door. He introduced himself to me as Dr. Metzenbaum, and I shook his soft hand.

"I need to talk with your father," he said. "Later on you and I can sit down and figure out what we're going to do with you." He smiled that kind of smile that adults use when they're trying to be friendly with strange kids, but I got the distinct impression that my presence at Metzenbaum's sanatorium wasn't something that pleased him all that much.

"Growing boy like you, I'll bet you're hungry. Go back to that building." He pointed through the screen at the building where I had slept. "You'll find a dining room. Have yourself some breakfast. Don't worry," he added, "you're part of our little family now. You'll figure out our routine quickly, I'm sure."

"Run along, Tommy," my father said.

As I walked back across the shaded lawn, I began to feel for the first time the isolation that my father's disease would impose on us. It was apparent that we would spend a great deal of time apart from each other and that Dr. Metzenbaum would dictate the routine of our lives. The grandness of the movie set gave way to a sense of foreboding. I wanted this part of my life to go quickly. I missed the streets and houses of the city.

Before I was finished eating, Dr. Metzenbaum joined me. He explained that tuberculosis was a disease that could be transmitted from one person to another through the air, so I wouldn't be able to spend a lot of time with my father. I would have the run of the grounds, but I was to stay out of the cottages and away from the hospital portion of the main building.

"Your father says you're a resourceful young man. Do you like the outdoors?

I nodded.

"Well, there's certainly a lot of that around here." He laughed at what was supposed to be a joke. "We're not used to having the child of a patient here. It's a new experience for us. It'll take some time to figure out how this is going to work."

Apparently Dr. Metzenbaum didn't have a clue as to what to do with me. I would be on my own.

After breakfast I found some books on tuberculosis on a shelf in the staff lounge. There was an old couch and a table with an assortment of mismatched chairs, a scratched and discolored refrigerator, and a hot plate that was rarely used as far as I could tell. Sometimes a nurse would come in with a cup of coffee from the kitchen down the hall. At first, they treated me like a kid brother, fawning over me, asking if I wanted ice cream or quizzing me about my father and my mother; but after a week I blended in, and I spent a lot of time reading up on tuberculosis.

Once, Dr. Metzenbaum came in, and when he saw what I was reading, he said, "Oh, planning on becoming a doctor, are you?"

I found out that history was full of people who had the same disease as my father: Thoreau, Keats, Shelley, Robert Louis Stevenson, Chopin, Emerson, Rousseau, Goethe—the list went on and on. Some books said tuberculosis heightened creativity, others that it dampened it. Some said it created an increased sexual desire, others that the sufferer wanted not much more than to sleep away his or her life. In a book called *The White Plague*, I read that Edgar Allan Poe's teenage wife suddenly clutched at her throat during a party, coughed, and a stream of blood spilled out of her mouth. Such an event was called a hemorrhage, and I had this vivid picture of a beautiful teenager, her skin as white as a handkerchief, with brilliant crimson cascading like a thin waterfall over her lips, down her chin, covering her throat and breasts.

My father had never, to my knowledge, coughed up blood, nor, I would soon learn, had any of the men in his cottage, although they all talked about it, carefully examining the stuff they hawked up into little paper sputum cups so that the nurse could measure the amount and look for blood.

An Indian nurse named Opal lived in a room at the end of the hall where I was placed. The hallway was shaped like an "L" and I discovered that if I climbed on a chair I could see out of my small high window down into the window of her room. She was a skinny girl, probably eighteen, and I immediately fell in love with her. Whenever she disappeared into her room, I went into mine, dragged the chair under the window, and climbed up to watch for her. During the day there was no point in looking since I couldn't see into her room, but in the evening when it was dark out and the lights were on, I could see a pie-shaped wedge of room that included the edge of her bed. I would hold onto the sill of the window with both hands, my face just above it, waiting, and sometimes the light went out without ever seeing her, but occasionally she sat on the edge of the bed, twice in panties and bra, and once without any clothes on. One night I caught a brief glimpse of her pubic hair and her tiny breasts with large dark nipples, and I was conscious, for the first time, of growing hard and knowing what it was all about.

The next morning I followed her into the staff room and, screwing up my courage, spoke to her.

"Are you married?" I asked.

She turned from the hot plate where she was heating water for tea.

"What kind of a question is that?"

"I just wondered," I said, feeling stupid, and at the same time trying to imagine her without any clothes on.

"No," she said. "Who the hell would I meet in a place like this? They're all about a hundred years old and they're sick."

"I'm not a hundred years old and I'm not sick," I said in a flash of what I thought was brilliance.

She smiled. "You're kinda cute," she said.

I felt the blood pounding in my ears.

"How old are you?"

"Fifteen," I lied. I knew I couldn't get away with eighteen. Fifteen was stretching it beyond belief.

"No, you're not," she said, pouring water into a thick white hospital mug and jiggling a tea bag up and down.

"Come back in about six years." She tousled the hair on my head with her other hand,

I felt really stupid.

3

MOST OF METZENBAUM'S WORKERS came from a small village nearby, and it took me only a few days to find where it was. It required a two-mile hike on a dirt and gravel road that wound over the ridge behind the sanatorium and then down a steep grade in the open sun. I set out late in the morning and by the time I got to Vallecitos, it was hot. The sun was straight overhead and there was no breeze. I wanted something to drink and I wanted some shade. My head felt woozy and my eyes ached. Vallecitos wasn't much, but it was the only town between the sanatorium and Williams, twenty miles north. The town clung to the hillside, the road separating a string of houses on the down side from the store, a church, and a lot with several house trailers with peeling paint on the sides. A dog came out into the road as if he were trying to menace me, but he was too hot to do more than growl and he lay down in the dust next to a telephone pole, his tongue hanging out, his sides heaving.

The slope behind the houses glittered in the sun, thousands of points of sharp light reflecting what seemed like countless jewels, some red, some blue, others glinting like diamonds. It took me a minute to realize it was broken glass, what must have been the remnants of thousands of broken bottles scattered down the slope. The front of the store had a small wooden porch that ran the length of the building, and sitting on the porch in cast-off chairs, their scuffed cowboy boots hooked into the rungs, were three young men. They were Indians.

One had a round face with skin that was brown and smooth as polished leather. Even though he was sitting down, I could tell he was a big man with a belly that hung over his belt. The second man was lean, with darker skin. He looked almost Spanish, but his hair was long and dark and pulled into a single braid at the back, like a horse's tail. The third man's face was pockmarked and he would have looked scary, but he had a huge grin as he watched me approach.

"Hey, you better get out of the sun before you cook," he said to me.

"I think maybe he's cooked already," said the big man. "He looks pretty much done to me."

"Naw," said the skinny guy. "I think he needs another ten minutes on this side. Then we better turn him around and walk him back to Messinbombs. Get him done on the other side."

I went up onto the porch and into the store. Inside it was darker and for a moment I couldn't see anything. Then I saw the cooler next to the cash register, a red metal chest with slots in the top and soda pop bottles up to their necks in cold water. I got out a dime, slipped it into the coin box at the end of the chest, and slid a bottle of Dr. Pepper along the slot until it came free at the end. Lifting it, dripping and cold, I pressed the bottle to my hot cheeks.

When I came out into the sunlight the three men were still there. I sipped at the bottle of Dr. Pepper and squinted at the light. I could feel them watching me. I sat on the single step, the bottle warming in my hands. One of them spoke.

"What you doing at Messinbombs, kid?"

I half turned to face him.

"You visiting somebody?" The man with the pockmarked face asked.

"No, I live there with my father."

"He some kind of a doctor?"

"No, he's a patient."

"You a lunger, too?"

It was the first time I heard that word. I would grow accustomed to it in the months ahead.

"No."

Pockmark continued to look at me but the other two were watching him, as if they were waiting to hear what he would say next.

And then it came out of me, a blurted question whose answer was apparent before it was asked: "Are you Indians?"

Pockmark slapped his leg. He turned to the other two and said in mock seriousness, "You an Indian? You? Me?" He faced me again. "What gives you that crazy idea, kid? You see our war ponies out back when you come down the road?"

"I've never seen Indians," I stammered. Then I added, "except in movies and in books."

"Where the hell you come from?"

"Chicago."

"Big city boy. Well, what do you think?" He turned again to his companions. "Shall we scalp him now or just tie him to a stake until the cavalry comes and kills us all off?"

"Lay off, Chief," said the big man. "He's a kid."

Pockmark looked at me again. "You got a champion here in Tiny. What's your name, kid?"

"Tom Hall."

"Well, Tom Hall, we are genuine Indians who have escaped from the reservation and are waiting for a call from Hollywood so we can get jobs as Indian scouts in Tom Mix movies. How's that?" he said to the big man. He tipped his chair back against the wall. One chair leg was bent inward and I wondered why it didn't collapse. I could see an immense buckle on his belt, bright silver inlaid with soft blue stones.

"What's your name?" I asked.

"I'm the Chief."

"Chief what?" and then, because I was nervous and didn't want to sound nosy, I added, "Is there more to it?"

"Chief Standing Buffalo Fart," said the big man with a grin. "That's about it, ain't it, Chief?"

Pockmark continued to smile. "And he," he said, pointing to the big man, "is named Large Man Who Squashes His Enemies Like Bugs."

"How about me?" the lean-faced man said.

"You," continued Pockmark, "are named He Who Stands in His Own Puke and Pisses."

At that the three of them began to laugh uproariously.

"My grandfather," said the lean-faced man between gasps of laughter, "was named One Who Pisses On White Guys When He's Drunk." And he bent double, his laugh now a high-pitched whinny.

"Jesus," said the big man. "We ain't gonna get any of them Hollywood actor jobs like you want unless we change our names," and the laughter rose again.

They paid no more attention to me and I finished my soda, left the bottle on the counter in the dark interior of the store, and started the long walk back to the sanatorium.

Each time over the next few weeks when I returned to Vallecitos I found the three of them on the porch of the store and I came to know more about them. The big man, called Tiny, was the gentlest of the three. The one with the pock-marked face was named Sleeping Jesus but nobody called him that—just Chief. And the third, the man with the lean Spanish face and the black ponytail, was Willie. Sometimes I watched while they worked on one of the old cars that littered Vallecitos, and I found out why so many of the cars rested on their sides or were upside down like abandoned desert tortoises. To avoid crawling in the dirt under the car to take out a transmission or a drive shaft or the leaf springs, they simply turned it on its side, scavenging parts here and there to make another car run. They never seemed to run for long. Whenever they got a car running, they disappeared for several days, but I never found out where they went.

Willie had lots of nieces and nephews, a few of them my age, and I hung around the Indian houses in Vallecitos, sometimes staying to eat Indian tortillas, soft pancakes of Indian bread rolled with chilies and stew inside. We played in the old car bodies, pretending to drive, or shot slingshots at ground squirrels. Once I spent an hour in an old Nash with a niece named Yolanda. I played the part of the doctor from the sanatorium examining her for signs of TB and spent most of the time getting her to unbutton her blouse so I could press my ear against her budding breasts and then began to use a technique I had seen Dr. Metzenbaum use, tapping my fingers against her ribs and pretending to listen intently. I was working my way toward the base of her belly when one of her brothers discovered us and threatened to beat the shit out of me if I ever touched his sister again. She seemed disappointed.

One afternoon Willie, Tiny, and the Chief dragged a motorcycle that belonged to Willie up onto the mesa. It had no clutch so the three of them propped up the back wheel, fired it up, and then the Chief sat on it while the other two pushed it off the blocks. It hit the ground, rear wheel throwing gravel, the bike lurching as he tried to keep it under control. It seemed to have only one speed and that was fast. There were shouts of "Ride 'em, Indian!" and the other two, with me tagging far behind, took off running while the Chief careened around scrub piñons and shot through buck brush until he ran out of gas. Willie, when it was his turn, sat back and hooked the heels of his cowboy boots over the handlebars, steering that way while hanging onto the ragged seat with both hands. His ride ended with a spectacular crash when the bike hit some rocks, and we rushed to drag him away while they yanked the spark wire loose to kill the still-whirling drive wheel.

The second time we dragged the motorcycle onto the mesa, Tiny asked if I wanted to have a ride. I remembered Willie lodged in the bushes while the engine roared, the wheel spinning and kicking up rocks. But I didn't want to appear as if I were afraid. I shrugged my shoulders.

"Come on, kid," he said. You don't need to go fast. Give it a try." He poured a cupful of gas into the tank, then lifted the back of the bike while the other two put a piece of stump under the frame.

I climbed over the seat, straddling it, and grabbed the grips.

"Turn this one if you want to go faster," he said. He kicked down on the starter and the motorcycle came to life. It rattled and shook as if it were about to come apart.

"Ready?" Tiny shouted above the engine.

I nodded. I was terrified.

"Bombs away!" the Chief yelled, and he gave the stump a kick. The motorcycle came down with a thump and I was nearly jerked off backwards. But in grabbing the handlegrips harder, I twisted them, and the bike shot forward at full speed, swerving from side to side. I had no control. A bush loomed in front of me and I turned the motorcycle, only to find I was headed toward the edge of the mesa. I could hear shouts of "Turn the sonofabitch!" and I laid the bike over on the other side. Somehow it righted itself and I jolted down into a small ravine, slamming forward over the handlebars. The effect was that I twisted the grip in the opposite direction and the bike slowed. I managed to turn it back toward the now small three figures who were waving their hands in the air. As they got bigger I could hear them whooping and one of them called out, "Ride 'em, whiteboy!"

But my sudden elation was short-lived. The bike hit some roots, slewed to one side, and went down. I felt my leg pinched between the motorcycle and the sandy ground and a hot pain shot through it. The engine continued to roar and the wheel caught something, sending the motorcycle pinwheeling off of me. Before it could lurch back, Tiny had me, one hand grabbing a fistful of my hair, the other my belt, and he hoisted me out of the way. The others shut down the bike and the silence was absolute.

"You okay, kid?" Tiny asked, setting me upright. My scalp tingled and I had the sudden impression of what it might have been like to have been scalped. But the tingling was replaced by the pain that welled up in my right leg. My trouser leg wasn't torn but when I lifted my pants I saw that the side of my calf was an angry red. Apparently I had come in contact with the exhaust pipe.

"Holy Jesus," Willie said. "That don't look so good." I rode down off the mesa on Tiny's shoulders, while Willie and the Chief dragged the motorcycle between them. Willie kept saying, "We're gonna get it. Messinbomb ain't gonna be happy we got this kid burned."

"Don't worry," I said. "I won't tell him."

"How you gonna get that fixed up, then?"

"I'll get one of the nurses to give me something," I said. "It's not broken or anything. It's just a burn." But I was on the verge of tears, the pain was so intense.

"I think," Tiny said from underneath me, "that we need a new name for the kid. How about we call you Flying Motorcycle?"

"More like Chief Crash and Burn," said the Chief.

"Okay by me," Tiny said. "From now on you're Crash and Burn."

I had only been in the West four weeks and I already had an Indian name. For a moment the pain in my leg disappeared.

By the time I had hobbled back to Metzenbaum's, the pain was so intense that I could barely stand it. Several times along the road I stopped to sob uncontrollably, but I managed to wipe off the dust and tears and walk reasonably upright to the staff room where I collapsed on the couch. Grace was the first one to come in. She was a middle-aged woman who lived in Vallecitos. I don't think she was a real nurse, but she wore the same white uniform that the others did and I told her what had happened.

"Please don't tell Dr. Metzenbaum," I said. "He won't let me go back to Vallecitos."

"Goddam those three," she said. "They're always messing something up." She looked at my leg where the skin had now risen in transparent blisters. "This don't look good," she said. She left the room and came back with Larry, the other nurse.

"Grace tells me you tried to tame a wild motorcycle," he said. He motioned for me to take off my pants. When I hesitated, he turned to Grace. "Find something to do," he said. "And the less said about this, the better."

Larry washed my leg and smeared a clear jelly on it, wrapping it with gauze. It immediately felt better, although it still throbbed.

"This is going to hurt a lot," he said. "It's going to scab over and we'll have to change that dressing twice a day. With any luck all you'll have is a nice scar to remind you."

"You won't tell Dr. Metzenbaum, will you? Or my father?"

He watched while I struggled to get the leg of my pants over the gauze-covered leg without putting pressure on it.

"You won't help your father get well by getting yourself hurt, you know."

"I know."

"This isn't much of a place for you, is it?"

"No, it isn't," I said, without thinking. Then I retreated. "It's okay. We aren't going to be here very long anyway."

"I hope not," he said and he ran his hand through my hair the way my mother used to do, but it felt different and I wondered where my mother was at that moment.

4

THE FIFTH WEEK I WAS at Metzenbaum's, I had my first x-ray. It was in a small, high-ceilinged room, everything painted the same shade of almost-green. The x-ray operator, who only came up the mountain once a month, was there when I arrived and he told me to take off my shirt. I felt nervous and exposed. He told me to stand with my chest against a glass-plated cabinet on the wall and hook my chin over the top. He pulled my arms out to my sides until I was spread-eagled against the glass. I heard him move away and then his muffled voice came from somewhere behind me.

"Take a breath and hold it."

I sucked in my breath and waited. There was a click and a grinding sound. I thought of Buck Rogers and his space ship and my lungs wanted to burst. It seemed to take forever.

Finally I heard him say, "Okay," and I let the air out of my lungs in a rush.

"You can put your shirt back on," he said, busy behind a partition at the back of the room. Overhead a huge contraption hovered over a long table that looked like the kind of table Dr. Frankenstein might have used. Pipes and cables snaked from the contraption over the top of the partition.

The x-ray machine was the only modern thing about Metzenbaum's. A staple of the doctor's treatment was something called "ethyl ester of chaulmoogra oil by intramuscular injection."

"Chaulmoogra oil sounds like a snake oil from one of your western stories, Tommy," my father said when I told him about it. "Are you sure you heard that right? He hasn't tried it on me yet."

All of the patients were required to take "heliotherapy" each afternoon which, as far as I could see, meant they sat in the sun with their clothes on. Mostly the regimen of the sanatorium consisted of careful attention to diet, exercise, and worry.

All of the patients kept a day-book of notations of the number of minutes they were out of bed; the amount of water they drank; the temperature of the day; the wind and weather; their own temperatures morning, noon, and evening; and, above all, they were continually told not to worry. "A great boon to health is a cheerful soul," was one of the things that Metzenbaum often said. But it seemed the more he said it, the more patients worried about not getting well.

A few of the patients who were felt to be near recovery were allowed to ride in the panel truck to Williams on Wednesdays. They usually carried with them a list of things other patients needed, but there were few things to need on Dr. Metzenbaum's mountain.

During rest periods in the mid-morning and afternoon there were absolute rules: no one was to speak or whisper, nor to rattle papers, nor could anyone do what was called "fancy work." Most of the patients, including the men, had an embroidery hoop they used to stitch designs for pillow covers or little decorative cloths. It was a strange sight to see a group of men sitting in a half-circle in the sun with their embroidery hoops silently slipping needles through the stretched cloth, several spools of colored thread in their laps. Embroidery was permitted during heliotherapy, but forbidden during the rest periods. Anything of that nature was "fancy work."

I was constantly being admonished by nurses and patients for running. When I protested that I wasn't sick, I was reminded that my pace might be upsetting to people who were forbidden to move faster than a walk.

I found a copy of Dr. Metzenbaum's admission rules in the staff room. It was part of a letter that he mailed out to prospective patients, so I knew that my father must have received one. Part of it read:

Bring a long warm bathrobe, slippers and soft head covering
All shoes must be fitted with rubber heels
You will be expected to make your own bed, assist in minor
* household duties and will be responsible for your quarters*
Each patient must have his own thermometer (available for 75 cents)
Bed patients will be charged $75 per month
Up-patients will be charged $45 per month
All bills will be payable on the first of month in advance
A chest x-ray must be provided upon admission or one will be
* taken at a charge of $1*

There were some other paragraphs praising the high altitude and clean dry air of Arizona and the modern cottages and dining facilities and the fact that the laundry was done in a "modern, fully-equipped laundry right on the grounds," but I later learned that the laundry in Williams refused to handle the sheets and towels of people who had tuberculosis. It occurred to me that the Williams laundry must accept the handkerchiefs from people who were blowing snot into them, so what was the difference? At Metzenbaum's, everybody was provided with little paper handkerchiefs and paper cups to spit in and these were burned in the stove each morning and afternoon.

This was, I would discover, part of the incredible isolation that Metzenbaum's colony of tuberculars felt. They were cut off from the rest of the world and for several hours a day even cut off from each other, forced to tie themselves with invisible ropes to the identical white-sheeted, white-blanketed beds that filled each cottage. It was no wonder the nurses told me to walk and patients snapped at me when I ran past a cottage. And now that the burn on my leg forced me into inactivity, I began to feel the oppression of the sanatorium. Time no longer mattered. Watches and clocks were put away since there was no need for them. The schedule was inviolable, always the same. And, unlike a broken leg or the flu, there seemed to be no visible horizon for tuberculars. My leg was scabbing over quickly and I couldn't wait to get back to Vallecitos. There I was Chief Crash and Burn. Here I was only an irritation.

5

THERE WERE DOGS IN VALLECITOS. They climbed on the roofs of the low buildings, lay about on the tops of sheds, and sat on the roofs of abandoned cars in the front yards of the ramshackle dwellings. Nondescript, their ribs showing, they barked at people, birds, passing clouds. It was impossible to walk through Vallecitos without raising a racket. I thought of them as Indian dogs, on the lookout for cavalry scouts. And, since I was white, that made me the enemy, and I tried hard to sneak past these sentries without being discovered; but they always found me out, first one and than another, until a whole chorus of discordant and chaotic yapping filled the village. It always took a long time to die down, settling at first, then rising again when one dog continued, the others joining in until from somewhere in the village would come a Goddammitshutupyoufuckingdogs! And the barking would abruptly halt.

Scrawny, long-legged, the dogs walked on their toes, tails up, stopping only to hump their backs, raise a hind leg and scratch vigorously at fleas, then trot along again, veering suddenly to right or left as if pulled by strings, but always alert. They were mostly the color of dirt with faces that had a touch of rat or coyote and they seemed attached to no one, although every house had at least one dog.

We had a dog for a short while in Chicago. It was a black cocker spaniel and unlike the Vallecitos dogs, it had a soft face and a vacant look as if it weren't very bright. In fact, my father said it had to go when it repeatedly left a little pile next to the door after it began to snow, unwilling to do its business on the icy sidewalks or the snow-covered vacant lot next door. My mother brought the dog home, but its fur got matted and it smelled and wasn't much of a companion for my sister and me, although that was why, my mother insisted, she had gotten it. I think it was one of my mother's impulses. She would suddenly do something like bring home a dog and then a few days later, lose interest in it.

Even though the dog refused to do its business outside, it played with us in the vacant lot where we lay on our backs in the snow and swept our arms and legs back and forth to make snow angels. It barked and growled and ran in circles when we threw snowballs as if it were deranged and then it flopped in the snow breathing heavily and my sister and I would have to carry the heavy wet thing inside where it lay in a steaming pile next to the door.

That winter my father worked at Washington Park where the trotters ran no matter how cold it was.

The dog disappeared. It was gone one day and when I asked my mother she said ask your father, and when I asked him he said it would be happier in a house with a yard to play in. I imagined it with some wealthy family in Oak Park learning to do tricks and being taken for walks along the elm-shaded streets by a maid.

That dog was not the first disappearance of my life. My father's work meant that we moved from one track to another as the racing seasons changed. Friends and houses came and went and the only constant things in my life were my father, my mother, and my sister. Now my mother and my sister had disappeared, too. I tried to imagine the kind of house they had found in Kentucky, but the houses always either looked like our last house in Chicago or the cottage my father lived in at Metzenbaum's. It was as if they were characters in a book I had read but had not finished and they, too, were half-finished and something more would happen to them that I could not know because I had lost the book and there was no way to find out how it ended.

6

LITTLE DRUM TAPS ON the chest with his fingers. Percussion, it was called. Metzenbaum moved the tips of his curved fingers from place to place in a pattern, pausing to tap, sometimes repeating the taps in the same spot, a faraway look on his face, listening to the resonant tone echoing from inside the chest cavity. He followed his tappings with his stethoscope, two long tubes that he stuck in his ears while he pressed the other end, a shiny metal disc, against the patient's chest or back. I watched him do this to Sam on a Wednesday morning in my father's cottage.

I found an old stethoscope in a closet in the staff room and I asked Dr. Metzenbaum if I could use it. He smiled and said that as long as I only listened to myself, it would be all right. He called me "the little doctor." I listened to my own chest. I was surprised to hear the wind of my breath rush in and out and my heart pound like the piston of an engine, and I found that if I pressed the stethoscope to a wall it magnified sounds so that I could make muffled voices on the other side understandable.

That was how I discovered that Opal had a man who slipped into her room late at night in violation of Metzenbaum's rules.

There was a utility closet next to her room and I found that I could sneak in and use my stethoscope to eavesdrop on her.

Her little cries were like squeaks made by a rubber mouse and I could hear his urgently whispering voice telling her to be quiet.

Then his voice would stop and it would be quiet and she would start up again, little gasping squeaks that came rhythmically through the wall, and I tried to imagine what they were doing, the squeaks louder until his voice, insistent, "Be quiet. Someone will hear you," and her reply, "I can't help it."

I wanted to know what was happening, listened to every noise, tried to catalog and organize footsteps, bed creaks, drawers opening and closing, snatches of conversation, although most of the time they spoke in soft voices barely audible even with my stethoscope pressed hard to the wall and the earpieces firmly in my ears.

I thought about asking my father, but I knew he wouldn't approve of my clandestine snooping and he'd want to know how I had heard the voices and noises. Besides, it wasn't the kind of thing we could easily talk about. I knew it had to do with sex, but she would sometimes urgently ask him to "come inside me now," and he would say "no, not yet," so I was pretty sure it wasn't the ordinary stuff people did that had been vaguely explained to me in a roundabout way once when I broached the subject to my mother.

My father was not a toucher. I cannot remember him holding me or putting his arm around my shoulder or playing catch with me or taking me fishing or any of the other things that fathers did in books I read.

It wasn't that he was a cold man or that he didn't care for me. I know he did. I felt close to him and knew he was my father.

Nor did my mother and father touch each other that much although she was the one who was demonstrative and she embarrassed him when she laughed too loudly or told stories or sometimes ran her fingers through his hair when he was talking.

When she told other people about things that had happened to the four of us, she added details and included conversations that I knew had not occurred. She would make our Sunday picnic in the Forest Preserve sound like an exotic adventure, her voice breathless with stray dogs that must have been rabid and brooks that rushed in a torrent, although I remembered them as trickles with worn banks that wound through the shabby picnic grounds. My father would sometimes try to correct her, but she only plowed ahead. For her, the truth was merely a starting place, a springboard from which she could take dives filled with somersaults and jackknifes into water so blue that only the rich could afford to swim in it.

She came from Kentucky. They had met at a racetrack. That much I knew.

Sometimes I wondered why she so willingly left me with my father; if she had seen something of him in me or perhaps his sickness had touched me, too, and in leaving the both of us she had, in fact, left only him.

Mostly I tried not to think of her and by the time we had settled into the routine at Metzenbaum's she had become a hazy memory. I found it hard to conjure up her face although her voice and her laugh were easy to recall.

I asked my father if he had a picture of her and he showed me a photograph he had in his wallet of the two of them at Arlington Park, my mother with both arms around his neck, a small piece of paper clutched in her hand.

"What's she holding?" I asked.

"A winning ticket. She hit a long shot and we suddenly had a hundred dollars." He touched her image with his forefinger and traced a circle around the two of them.

He smiled. "We sure were rich that day."

"Did she bet on all the races?"

`"No. Your mother used to bet two dollars on the last race. She'd come out to the track at the last race and afterwards wait for the tellers to balance out. Earl Joyner took the picture. Then the three of us went out and celebrated. Earl was the clubhouse runner. Remember him?"

I nodded my head, yes.

"You would have been pretty small. The picture was taken before you and Pamela came along."

I nodded again. Earl Joyner was one of the few people who had ever come to our house, a tall man with nicotine-stained fingers who did card tricks for me and my sister.

"Why did you want to see a picture of your mother?"

"I just wanted to be reminded of what she looked like."

"Do you want to keep this for a while?"

"No."

"You're sure?"

"Yes. I just wanted to look at her face."

He put the photograph carefully into his wallet. "Do you miss her?" he asked.

"I don't think so," I said. "It seems like we knew her a long time ago."

"You'll see her again." He placed his wallet on the shelf at the head of his bed. He set it perfectly between his upright shaving brush and his little clock, then touched it with the ends of his delicate fingers as if to make sure it was in line with the other two objects. Somehow, in that gesture, I could understand why my mother was gone, but if I had been asked to explain it, no words would have come.

"When I'm well again," he said, "you'll see. Now you'd better get a move on before Metzenbaum finds you sitting on my bed."

7

WE HAD COME IN THE heat of the late summer. After the noon meal the sanatorium grounds became silent, the temperature climbed to nearly a hundred degrees. Heat shimmered from the gravel walks and crackling little pops came from the pine forest when expanding pockets of pitch exploded like tiny firecrackers. The turpentine smell of hot pines filled the air. Nothing moved. I would explore the sanatorium during those hot hours after the noon meal, knowing that everyone had gone to cottage beds or cooler rooms, shades drawn against the yellow air. In each cottage, four patients lay on their beds. In the main building nurses napped; the Indians and Mexicans who worked in the kitchen and outside disappeared. Metzenbaum sat in his half-darkened office, reading at his big desk, his white smock hanging on a peg behind him, looking more like a farmer or someone's grandfather in his shirtsleeves.

On one of those afternoons I met Mrs. Green

In the kitchen Manuel was chopping onions. He had a clothespin pinching his broad nose and he wore a white sleeveless undershirt, his brown arms and shoulders slick with sweat. He was a short man with a belly and he would make sandwiches for the two of us, flat rounds of corn tortilla, soft and chewy with thick slices of cold ham slathered with mustard, and sometimes he piled refried beans on the ham before wrapping the tortilla. He chopped little green chili peppers into the mixture and they made my eyes water. The ham was the only thing I recognized that had appeared on Metzenbaum's tables.

"Messinbomb feed this to them lungers they maybe get better," he would say. "They all too skinny."

When I said that they were skinny because of the TB, he laughed. "You eat lots of them chilies," he said. "They clean you out good. Then you fill up on beans and tortillas. You be okay."

I was on my way from the kitchen with my tortilla when I passed Mrs. Green's room. It was the required rest period and I caught a quick glimpse of her on the bed, eyes closed, apparently asleep; but as I slid past the open door I heard her voice call out, "You! Young man! Stop right where you are. Let me see you!"

I backed up cautiously until I was in the center of the doorway. She had turned her head and was looking out the door.

"What are you doing skulking around at this hour?"

"Nothing."

"Nonsense. Nobody does nothing," she said in a voice that reminded me of Miss Higginbothan, my second grade teacher. Mrs. Green was tall, an angular woman who filled the length of the white frame bed, and she seemed not much older than my father. Her head was surmounted by an incredible swirl of hair the color of straw, wound in interlaced ropes intricately knotted within itself. It struck me that it must take hours to construct, and then I remembered that all of the patients seemed to have things they did that took hours. One of my father's cottage mates worked puzzles that had a thousand pieces and consisted mostly of sky and formless clouds, and when he finished a puzzle he wordlessly dumped it into a paper sack, dipped his hand into the sack for a piece and deliberately began again.

"I haven't seen you before," Mrs. Green said. "Who are you?"

"Tom Hall," I replied.

"Speak up," she commanded. "Don't mumble. It isn't becoming in a man."

"Thomas Hall," I said again, louder.

"Are you one of us?" she asked and I wasn't sure what she meant. Then I realized she was asking if I were a patient.

"No, my father is. He's in one of the cottages."

"What are you doing here? This is no place for a boy."

"I don't have any place else to be," I said, and as soon as I said the words, the finality of what I was saying came to me. I really didn't have any place else to be. I was as much a part of Metzenbaum's colony of sick people as they were.

And that began my mornings with Mrs. Green. She made an arrangement with Dr. Metzenbaum so that I would come just after breakfast to her doorway. I sat in a chair and she taught me from her bed. Never mind that it was still late summer when school would have been out for me in Chicago. She would teach me French, I would report on books that I was reading, and there would be geography lessons. There would be no need for science or mathematics, she said, since they were sterile disciplines fit only for the narrow-minded.

The arrangement seemed to please everyone. Since the sanatorium was carefully organized around the daily prescribed schedule, my planned mornings fit more easily into Dr. Metzenbaum's world than being entirely footloose. I had, without knowing it, been a loose cannon on deck, as Mrs. Green put it.

French was done orally, with Mrs. Green speaking phrases and me repeating them. Her agreement with Dr. Metzenbaum was that I was to do most of the talking, but quick-minded Mrs. Green was never satisfied with my performance. "Again," she would command, making me repeat until the phrase was satisfactory.

I selected books from the library, a shelf in the dining room filled with books that had been left by previous patients. Reading was one of the few things that patients were allowed to occupy their time. The bed-patients weren't allowed to do much else, and even the books were monitored by Metzenbaum, with mysteries or romances banned on the grounds that they would increase the pulse rate and thus defeat the idea of complete rest.

I used an old Goode's School Atlas for geography lessons, memorizing states, mountain chains, countries, and continents. These were the most interesting lessons. Mrs. Green would interrupt: "The Atlas Mountains. The Blue Men of Morocco. Mr. Green and I" (he was always referred to as 'Mr. Green') "saw them." And the indigo-skinned men in dark burnooses would appear in Metzenbaum's plain room. Mrs. Green would sheathe the walls with earth and the tea would become thick and dark. Together the three of us would walk down dark corridors of streets cut through the interiors of oasis buildings; we ate sweet dates, and a camel snorted its foul breath on us. We walked to the edge of the coolness and looked out into the hard brilliance of the desert sun where, Mr. Green said, wild men rode fast horses and bought and sold human beings.

Mr. Green was a purser for a steamship line in New York, she said, and when she was well again they would go back to North Africa where the air was so dry that things that died in the desert did not decay, but remained just as they were at the moment of death.

It wasn't until much later I learned Mrs. Green was a stage-three patient, which meant that she was given little chance for recovery. That, no doubt, was why Metzenbaum had bent the rules to allow her to violate the "Metzenbaum crawl," as the patients described life on the mountain. In each cottage was a small white placard with the words:

Never hurry
Walk very slowly
Speak in a modulated voice
Don't whistle or sing
Never speak to anyone more than ten feet from you
Never stand if you can sit down

I tried to conform, speaking softly, but Mrs. Green would demand that I speak louder and when I protested that loud voices were prohibited by Metzenbaum's rules, she would only snort, "Rules be damned! Full speed ahead! Name the longest river in North America!"

8

I THINK, BECAUSE I WAS TWELVE, I was ignored. I sat in the staff room and listened to them, learned about the disease and about sick people. After a while the talk lost for me my fear of being sick. It was like listening to a bunch of mechanics talk about cars or machines. By now I knew the names of many of the patients, although except for Dr. Metzenbaum, the men in my father's cottage, Mrs. Green, the cook and the nurses, I had little personal contact with them. But those names spoken in the staff room soon became like old friends to me. There were a few "stage-threes" or "terminals," as they called them—two men and Mrs. Green who were in the most advanced stages of the disease and were kept isolated from the rest of the patients. In fact, nobody ever referred to anyone as a 'patient.' They were just people who lived in this little village of the diseased in a cluster of wooden buildings on the shoulder of a mountain.

There were the "regulars" like my father and the men in his cottage. The nurses had other names for them. "Lungers" was the common name, used to distinguish those who had TB from people who didn't.

And there were the nurses—Opal, Larry and Grace who, like Larry, lived in Vallecitos. Gradually I learned that Opal was, in fact, more like an orderly, making up beds, cleaning up after patients, bringing food; while Larry and Grace were the ones who carried out Dr. Metzenbaum's orders.

Metzenbaum had a young doctor who assisted him, but Larry and Grace treated him with contempt in their conversations in the staff room, and an elaborate deference when he was present. I noticed that both Opal and Grace seemed to play second fiddle to Larry, who moved through Metzenbaum's little world with a sureness that had, at first, convinced me he was a doctor. I had never seen a nurse who wasn't a woman, but I hadn't had much contact with nurses and, although it seemed odd to me, it didn't seem odd to anyone else.

I wandered the grounds of the sanatorium until I was a familiar sight to patients who waved at me from inside their cottages. Rest time was when I explored, since everyone, nurses and patients, were expected to stay where they were, and I knew the hallways and grounds would be empty. I crept about Indian-fashion, making mental notes of who lived where and what each room or building was for. One afternoon I found myself in part of the main building that was new to me. Off a hallway was a small room with a microscope on a table and some test tubes and bottles of disinfectant. It smelled of the carbolic acid that was used to disinfect nearly everything in the sanatorium. I thought about going in but the room had an ugly laboratory look to it that made me uneasy.

Further down the hallway was a door that opened to a room with pale green walls and pale green wooden trim that had been painted many times and had the look of permanence. There was a large glass window in one wall and on the other side I could see a man in a bed. His eyes were sunken and the skin of his nose seemed stretched over the bone. He lay, looking at the ceiling, and I came closer to the window. I could not tell if he could see me. Suddenly he turned on his side, facing me, and began to cough convulsively. Through the window I could hear the coughs, faint and sluggish; watch his heaving body; and then came the blood. It came in a rush, spilling from his mouth onto the side of the bed and onto his bedclothes and down his chin, a red flood that stunned me. He reached down and took a fistful of sheet and rubbed the blood off his chin and from his lips and called out something, sinking back onto his pillow.

I had never seen such red. It was so bright, as if it were lit from within, brilliant, breathing light, fading as it was absorbed by the cloth on the bed.

Larry came into the room from a door at the right, quickly followed by Metzenbaum. They bent over the man, talking earnestly, and then Opal came in with a basin of water and washcloths. At that moment Metzenbaum turned to face the window and he saw me. He must have seen my stunned face, frozen in fascination, and he shouted at me, "What the hell are you doing there?" so loudly I could easily hear him through the glass. Then, to no one in particular, he shouted, "Who the hell let that kid in there? Will someone tell me who in the goddamn hell let that kid into that room?"

They all whirled to look at me and Metzenbaum turned and left the room, only to reappear almost immediately in the doorway of the green room where I was standing.

"Do you know where you are?" he demanded. When I didn't answer, he said, "You have no business here! This is an isolation room. Dammit, I'm sick and tired of seeing you every time I turn around. You get the hell out of here and get to your room and you stay there until you're sent for!"

Behind him, Larry and Opal were shifting the thin man, lifting his body so they could remove the bloodied sheets and slip clean sheets beneath him. He seemed not to notice what they were doing. Metzenbaum's white smock had blood on it, like a butcher's apron. I was rooted to the floor, unable to move.

"Do you hear me?" Metzenbaum shouted. "Get your nosy little ass out of here this very instant!"

Opal was wrapping the bloody sheets into a ball. She dropped them onto the floor. The basin that Larry held was now filled with a pink liquid that, for some absurd reason, suddenly reminded me of the valentines I had cut out of construction paper when I was in the fourth grade. They were stripping the bloodied hospital gown off the man. He was terribly thin, his chest concave, his ribs showing. I expected his skin to be pale and white, but it was diffused and rosy, as if it were giving off heat. Tuberculosis was no longer four middle-aged men in a cabin at camp; it was bright blood and the concave chest of the thin man who was poised on the edge of death. The thin man's body was not unlike my father's body, and I wanted to see if my father was all right; but Metzenbaum's words rang in my ears and I bolted for the door.

I wove my way through the rabbit warren of hallways until I was at my own room where I shut the door and threw myself on the bed. The image of the blood was still with me. I had not known that blood could be so red or that someone could lose so much and still live. I had seen, I knew, a hemorrhage, something that I had read about in my books. But this wasn't the romantic imagining I had dreamed about when I pictured Poe's wife or the dying Stevenson in the South Pacific. This was brutally clinical. This was here and it was red and it came coughing up from the lungs of a thin man who could easily be my father, and I was afraid.

It was dark when Dr. Metzenbaum knocked on my door. I awoke, disoriented, thinking for a minute that I was in my room in the little house in Illinois. I heard Metzenbaum's voice again and I realized where I was. I wanted not to be there.

"Are you in there?"

The door opened and Metzenbaum peered in.

"Are you in here?" he asked again.

"Yes," I said, sitting up.

He flipped the light on and came into the room, leaving the door open into the hallway. He sat on the end of the bed and it sagged under his weight.

"Do you know what you saw today?" he asked.

"Yes."

"So, you tell me what it was."

"It was a hemorrhage."

"Quite the little doctor, aren't you?"

"No, sir."

"No, I think you are rather like a doctor. Most kids would have thrown up or run away, but you stood there and watched." He paused. Through the open doorway I saw Opal go past and could see her sneak a glance at the two of us.

"Did it frighten you?"

"Yes."

"That doesn't happen to everybody who has TB," he said.

I nodded.

"'The Captain of all these men of death that came against him to take him away was the Consumption, for it was that that brought him down to the grave.' John Bunyan wrote that nearly three hundred years ago. I don't suppose you know who John Bunyan was?"

"No."

"You're a bright kid. With you, I'm never sure." He placed his hand on my leg. It was pudgy and the fingers were puffy like little dough sticks. The nails were clipped short in perfect accordance with the ends of his fingers.

"They used to think that if you could be touched by a king it would cure you. Did you know that in *Macbeth* Shakespeare describes the king doing that? But there aren't any kings left around here."

Metzenbaum's voice seemed to come from a long way off and I began to feel somehow connected to him. I remembered my father saying that Metzenbaum didn't cure anybody. The old doctor seemed lost in thought. Then he raised his hand to my forehead, holding it there for a while. His fingers felt cool.

"You can't stay here," he said. "This is no place for a boy. I must have a talk with your father." He rose and went to the door. "It's past supper," he said. "Go down to the kitchen and get something to eat." He was wearing a clean smock, so starched and white that it seemed to shine in the hallway light.

9

I DIDN'T EXPECT THERE would be anyone except my father in the cottage. Wednesday afternoons Henry and Clifford and Sam were usually gone, Henry and Clifford to heliotherapy, which meant they lay for an hour in wicker lounge chairs on the southern slope of the grounds, and Sam to his weekly examination with Dr. Metzenbaum. But this afternoon as I approached the cottage I heard music and I could see two figures, close together, framed in the open window. I came slowly up to the cottage and could make out in the shadowy interior my father and someone else. They were dancing. I didn't go to the door, but went to the screened window next to it and carefully peeked over the edge of the sill. The other person was Larry, but he didn't have on his usual starched white shirt and pants. He was wearing light blue trousers and a shiny blue shirt with sleeves that hung loosely from his shoulders, tightly bunched at his wrists. Nobody at Metzenbaum's dressed that way. The patients dressed in plain-colored robes, and the doctors and nurses always wore their traditional white uniforms. The rest of the help wore dungarees and work shirts, so Larry's bright costume seemed just that: a costume among these drab camp dwellers, and when the two of them moved in the soft light from the open windows, I could see something glitter on the collar of the shirt, as if it were stitched with tiny electric wires.

The music was coming from a small portable record player that looked like a little suitcase open on my father's bed and several records were scattered next to it. I recognized the song. It was the Andrews Sisters singing "Don't Sit Under the Apple Tree with Anyone Else but

Me." My father looked flushed and hot as the song ended and he stood mopping his brow as Larry changed the record.

"You have to relax, Eddie," he was saying as he sifted through the records on the bed, put one on the turntable, and carefully set the needle down on it. It was a slow song by a band with lots of clarinets, and Larry went to my father, put one hand on his shoulder, the other on his waist, and said, "Flow with it, Eddie. Don't dance *to* the music. Dance *with* it."

My father put both hands around Larry's waist and the two of them began to move, my father looking down at his feet, then, as the clarinets soared, clasping his fingers just above Larry's belt. I watched, my heart pounding, imagining that they could hear it above the music; but they were oblivious to my face at the screen, Larry softly counting the steps, my father looking off at nothing in a dream-like state. When the song ended, they continued to stand in the same spot, gently rocking, although their bodies weren't touching, only their hands. They seemed to stay that way for a long time, the record still spinning, the rhythmic hissing of the needle keeping time with their bodies.

I thought about coughing or clearing my throat, but then I thought better of that, and slowly crouching down, I backed up until I could safely turn and run without being seen. I didn't stop until I was around the corner of the hospital building. I leaned against the wall in the hot sun, waiting, watching the buzzards lazily wheel over the canyon. I could smell the heat radiating from the paint and I listened carefully for the music from the record player, but I couldn't hear it. I began counting—one-thousand one, one-thousand two—until I reached a hundred, and then I went around the corner toward the cottage. This time I whistled a song, scuffing my feet in the gravel path. It wasn't until I reached the cottage door that I realized I was whistling the Andrews Sisters song.

I opened the door of the cottage and stepped inside as if it were any Wednesday afternoon. My father was sitting on his bed and Larry was bent over next to him, closing the little phonograph. The records were all in their jackets in a neat pile.

My father hit his head with the heel of his hand in mock astonishment. "It must be Wednesday. Here's Tommy!"

"Hi, Sport," Larry said, turning to look at me. "Your father and I were listening to records. Want to hear some?"

"No thank you," I said, standing there wondering what to say. Finally I said, "I've never seen you not in your uniform."

"What do you think?" he said, straightening and snapping his wrists so that the bloused sleeves jumped I could see now that the collar and the front of the shirt where the buttons were lined up were decorated by tiny glass beads stitched into the seams. "It's genuine Navajo," he said.

"Looks okay," I said.

He turned to my father. "'Looks okay.' Your son is a man of few words, Eddie." He turned to me again. "You're supposed to say, 'Looks great, Larry. I love a man with style.'"

I felt my face flush and he laughed.

"I think I've embarrassed your kid, Eddie." Nobody ever called my father anything except Edward or maybe Ed, but he didn't seem to mind, just sat there grinning, his forehead shining, his hands on his knees.

"I gotta be going," Larry said, picking up the phonograph by the handle on the case and scooping the records under his other arm. "Don't forget," he added.

"I won't. Thanks for coming by," my father said, looking at me.

Larry winked at me, looked at the door, then at me again. I realized he didn't have a free hand and leaped to open the door for him.

"See ya, Sport," he said, stepping out into the sunlight. The sun lit the shiny blue of his shirt and caught the glass beads, and it seemed for a moment as if it had caught fire. Then he disappeared around the corner of the hospital building.

My father was stretched out on his bed, staring at the ceiling. "I forgot it was Wednesday," he said.

"You want to play checkers?"

"No," he replied. "I think I'll rest for a while."

"You want me to go?"

"Good God, no," he said. "Stay and talk to me. Tell me what you've been doing. What's happening on the Magic Mountain. Tell me about your Indian friends." He turned his head to look at me.

"Did you see us dancing?" he asked.

"Yes," I said. "I came up before and heard the phonograph."

"I thought so," he said. "Maybe it was the song you were whistling. Or maybe I saw you. Were you at the screen?"

"Yes."

"Why didn't you say anything?"

"I didn't think I should." I wished he would change the subject.

"He was teaching me to dance. He used to be a professional dancer."

"You already know how to dance," I said. "I've seen you dance with Mom."

"There's always room for improvement, Tommy." He swung his legs over the side of the bed, sitting up.

"You like him?" he asked.

"Who?"

"Larry, of course. Come on, Tommy, don't play dumb. Tell me what you think."

"I think he's nice," I said, unable to figure out what he wanted me to say.

"He makes me feel alive."

"You are alive," I said. "Let's play checkers."

10

THE NEXT DAY WASN'T WEDNESDAY, but I wanted to talk to my father; so I did what I had done several times before when I had felt compelled to break the rule about limiting my contact with him. I wandered about the grounds with a book, waiting until I saw no one in sight, and then slipped up next to the wall of his cottage and pressed my face up to the screen above my father's bed. He was lying on the bed as I knew he would be and I whispered, "Dad?"

He turned his head toward the screen. "It's not Wednesday," he said in a soft voice. "What's wrong?"

"Nothing. I just wanted to talk to you."

"Only for a minute. I don't want Metzenbaum getting wind of this and taking away our Wednesday visits. Make it quick."

"What's your temperature today?" I asked.

"Ninety-nine point six," he said. Then he added. "It's always ninety-nine point six. Why do you ask me every time, Thomas?"

"Because one of these days it's going to be lower," I said confidently.

He didn't say anything, just lay there on his back in his white shirt and gray gabardine trousers, everything neatly pressed as if he were going someplace. The other men in his cottage wore old bathrobes and pajamas and scuffed about in slippers. But my father dressed each morning, then lay on his bed, his shoes neatly together at the side of the bed. He looked like he would swing his legs over the side in a minute, tie his shoes, and go off to work.

"Can I ask you something?" I lowered my voice so the other three men couldn't hear.

"You already asked me something," he said. He smiled. "Sure, go ahead. What's up?"

"I read in a book that you get tuberculosis from breathing in germs. How come the nurses don't get it?"

"Some of them do. That's why all the cottages have open windows so the air doesn't get filled with TB."

"Larry had his face next to yours. Won't he get it?"

My father sat up, bringing his face close to the screen . "Promise you won't breathe a word of this to anybody?"

"I never told anybody in Chicago that you had TB." I was afraid of what he was about to say, as if he would reveal some awful secret that I didn't want to know.

"Larry has it, too. But Dr. Metzenbaum doesn't know it. Nobody here knows about it except me." He paused. "And now you. He got it working here. He went to Phoenix and took a test and it turned out positive."

I was relieved that this was the secret, but it puzzled me that my father knew so much about Larry, who, up until then, had only been a man in a white uniform who glided through Metzenbaum's mountaintop bearing towels or bedpans, inserting thermometers, and carrying trays of food.

"Why doesn't he become a patient?"

"Because he says Metzenbaum doesn't cure anybody. He says Metzenbaum is a quack. Which is why we're leaving."

"When?"

"Not long. As soon as we can get Larry's car fixed."

"I didn't know he had a car."

"He does. It's a '39 Olds, but the clutch is worn out and we have to replace it before we can go. And this is where you come in."

"Where will we go?"

"I'll tell you on Wednesday," he said, propping himself on one elbow. He rolled his eyes toward the opposite side of the cottage and I understood he didn't want to say anything more with the others around. He lay back on his pillow.

"I have to trust you to do some things, Tommy," he said. "I can't go out and do them myself."

11

NOW LARRY TOOK ON a new interest for me. I wanted to find out everything I could about him. He was neither handsome nor ugly, but sort of in-between plain with a flat-top haircut that made him look like a boxer or a serviceman, and he carried himself with an assurance that bordered on the cocky—as if he were daring people to say something about him. The more I studied him, the more unlikely he seemed to be a nurse; yet the patients liked him and Dr. Metzenbaum favored him over the others, including the young doctor.

He wore a starched white shirt over a white undershirt and a pair of white pants that never seemed to lose their crease. He alternated a tiny red heart on the collar of his shirt with a pin which had the words *St. Mary's Hospital* on it. He wore a tiny silver dinosaur pin on the other collar.

Several days after I saw the two of them together in my father's cottage, I saw Larry again in Vallecitos. I had walked into town early that morning, not for any particular reason, but just to get away from the sanatorium; and as I came up the rise where the broken glass littered the hillside, a motorcycle came toward me. The rider had a white bandana wrapped around his face, a leather coat with long fringes that flew from the shoulders, and cowboy boots with sharp heels hooked over the footrests. It never occurred to me that it might be Larry.

He saw me and slowed the motorcycle, stopping to wait for me to approach, feet on the ground on opposite sides of the bike, the heavy motor rumbling. When I got close enough, he pulled the scarf down around his neck and I realized it was Larry.

I wasn't sure what to say. I had seen men on motorcycles before, but in Chicago they always seemed to be ridden by young men in black leather jackets or by solid old men like Mr. Pulaski down the street who rode his motorcycle to the packing plant every morning.

"Where you headed to so early, Sport?"

"To town." Then I added. "I didn't know you rode a motorcycle."

"Not bad, huh?" he said, running his hand over the shiny enamel of the gas tank between his legs, wiping off the thin film of dust. "What do you think?"

I didn't know what to think. I stood there in the morning heat, the bubbling noise of the motorcycle surrounding us, smelling of gas and oil and dust.

"Come on," he said. "I'll give you a ride." He patted the seat and slid forward, turning the motorcycle to face Vallecitos.

"Watch out for the tail pipe," he said, with a wink. "I guess you know what it can do."

I carefully climbed onto the seat behind him, keeping my leg wide of the hot pipe.

"Put your arms around me."

I gingerly encircled his waist. I wasn't sure what to do with my hands and I was hesitant to press myself to his back, but I felt his gloved hand press mine against his stomach.

"Ready?"

"Yes."

He twisted the handgrip twice, the motor roaring each time, and then he kicked something with his foot and we were off. I felt myself being thrown backward and I grabbed tightly to him, pulling my body close to his, my face buried in his shoulder, the wind whipping the fringes of his jacket against my face. I was the shell on a beetle's back and it was a few moments before I realized my eyes were tightly closed.

He stopped in front of the store where Willie, the Chief, and Tiny were sitting on the porch.

"Want a soda?" Larry asked.

"Sure," I said into his ear and he turned off the engine. As I climbed off the back, Willie called out, "Hey, looks like Chief Crash and Burn got hisself a boyfriend."

Larry leaned the motorcycle on its kickstand and peeled off his gloves. "I'll crash and burn you if you ever put him on that piece of shit of yours again."

"Whoa!" Willie said. "Touched a nerve there. How's about loaning us that bike of yours. It says Indian on the side of it. Must belong to some relative of ours."

"Touch it and you die," Larry said with a grin. "Come on, Sport."

We went inside and fished cold bottles out of the cooler.

"So," Larry said, "You're the famous Chief Crash and Burn."

I nodded.

"Next time those three crazy Indians want you to do something like that, you want to remember you don't want your name changed to Chief Crash and Die."

I nodded again.

"I'm not going to ride Willie's bike," I said. "Can I ask you something?"

"Sure."

"My dad says you think Dr. Metzenbaum is a quack."

"Maybe I was a little harsh. Metzenbaum tries hard. But mostly people who get better would have gotten better anyway. I've worked in three different sans and they're all pretty much the same." He pressed the cold bottle to his cheek and looked straight at me. "Metzenbaum's okay."

"Then why are we leaving?"

"Who said you were leaving?"

"My dad. He said we were going to fix your car and go someplace. Are you going, too?"

"Holy smoke, cat's out of the bag," he said. "You think it's a bad idea?"

It was the first time in all of the moves that I had made that anyone had asked me what I thought. How could I know if it was a bad idea when I didn't even know where we were going or why we had to leave Metzenbaum's. Obviously Larry was going with us. And he sure didn't look like he had TB.

"Where are we going?" I asked.

"I think your father ought to tell you," he replied, "Come on, I'll give you a ride back to the san."

We were moving again. I wondered what would happen if I announced that I wanted to stay in Vallecitos and become an Indian.

12

WHEN I CAME TO THE cottage the following Wednesday I was full of questions. I stood outside the screen next to my father's bed and he asked me what I had been doing, what book I was reading, what news I had found in my travels around the sanatorium. I was a break from the monotony of Metzenbaum's rigid rest schedule.

I told him about Willie, Tiny, the Chief, and Vallecitos, but I avoided too much detail and left out my wild motorcycle ride and the burn on my leg. I think he sensed I didn't tell him everything but he didn't press for more, only listened intently to my description of Tiny and the Chief tipping a car on its side using nothing but brute strength. He was pleased that Mrs. Green was giving me lessons and made me say some French phrases and translate for him.

"She must have led a fascinating life," he said. "Imagine going to North Africa and Europe."

When I asked him if he had ever gone any place like that, he said, "No. Your mother and I went to Michigan once and stayed in a cabin in the woods. It was one room and had a little stove in the middle, just like the one here, and it got so cold I had to keep getting up every hour to put more wood on it, and when we got up in the morning there was ice in the water glass on the drainboard. It was November, just before they closed for the winter. That was before you were born."

I tried to picture my father and mother in a little cabin in the north woods but it didn't fit. As far as I knew, he had always lived in the city and dressed like a man who wouldn't know how to feed a wood stove. It suddenly occurred to me that my father might be more interesting than I had imagined.

"Where are we going?" I blurted out.

"I'm not sure," he said. "But I need to find a better place than this. I need to find some place where they can cure me."

"Larry's going with us," I said.

"You figured that out?"

"No, he told me." Then I added, "sort of."

"Is that okay with you?"

"Sure, I like him."

"So do I. What else did he tell you?"

"Nothing. He said you'd tell me."

"We haven't decided anything yet. We need to get Larry's car fixed and we need to find a place that can do more than take my temperature and wait."

"When will we go?"

"A few weeks. Maybe a month. Don't worry. We'll lick this thing. Now you go find Mrs. Green and learn some more French. Who knows, maybe we'll all join the French Foreign Legion and go the Sahara and you can be our translator. They say the desert is good for lungers." He laughed, but it wasn't a funny kind of laugh. It was the kind of laugh that made me uneasy, as if it were a nasty joke that had been played on him.

But that day's lesson with Mrs. Green didn't happen.

Her door was open and when I looked in I saw an empty bed, stripped of the sheets. Opal was bustling about, putting things in a trunk: Mrs. Green's silver-framed photograph of her husband in his purser's uniform, her neatly folded clothes.

"Where is she" I asked. "Is she going home?"

"Nobody told you?" Opal said.

"No. Has she left yet?"

"You go find the nurse or Dr. Metz. I ain't the one to tell you."

"Tell me what?"

"Go on," she said. "I got work to do."

I found Dr. Metzenbaum in his office.

"Has Mrs. Green gone yet?" I asked

He turned in his wooden swivel chair to look at me. He seemed momentarily puzzled.

"Do you mean gone home, Thomas?"

"Yes," I said, but I was beginning to sense something was out of place.

"In a manner of speaking, she did." He placed his soft white hands on the arms of the chair. "She died last night."

"But I saw her yesterday. She was all right then."

"I'm afraid she wasn't all right, Thomas. She was very ill."

"Did she hemorrhage?" I thought of the man in the green room.

"Nothing like that. She just didn't wake up. Her body stopped fighting the disease and she gave up."

"But Mrs. Green wasn't a quitter!"

"Perhaps not."

"Will a relative come and get her?"

"No. She'll be buried in Williams." It was clear he was uncomfortable with my questions and wanted me to go someplace, but the problem with Metzenbaum's sanatorium was that there really was no place to go.

"Why don't you go to the kitchen and find Manuel and tell him I said you could have some ice cream with chocolate syrup," he said. Then he added, "These things happen, Thomas."

But Manuel wasn't in the kitchen and I prowled around until I found him at the back door of the isolation wing. He was loading a coffin into the back of Metzenbaum's panel truck, a long box of plain, unpainted wood. I tried to imagine Mrs. Green in the box, lying on her back, arms at her sides, but the thought of the dark ceiling only inches from her face made me shudder and I was glad when Manuel started the truck and drove off. I watched the trees across the canyon, waiting in the still afternoon until I could see the soft dust rising, revealing Manuel's descent down the mountain, a thin gray cloud like smoke from an old rubbish fire drifting through the hazy hot forest.

The sound of the engine came and went as he wound his way down the mountain and it was silent again, only a blue jay calling from somewhere, everything in the two o'clock heat waiting for the afternoon wind to come sighing through the trees. Mrs. Green was gone and I was still there. Manuel didn't look much like Metzenbaum's Captain of All These Men of Death, I thought.

13

BUT MY FATHER DIDN'T tell me the next Wednesday or the one after that. Two weeks passed without a mention of our leaving. He wasn't getting any better. Metzenbaum said to be patient, that these things have their ups and downs. "It's not just a steady climb up the ladder, you know."

My father seemed to have less energy, to lie on his bed throughout the day, too tired to move.

He said that the more tired his body felt, the more active his mind raced. "It feels like I'm on fire," he said. When I came on Wednesdays to the cottage now he talked continuously, a low intense voice no more than a stage whisper, even though we were the only two there.

He told me about a book he had read years before that had suddenly come back into his head. It was, he said, as if he were again reading the pages. It was a story that took place in an old stone house in France on a slope above the vineyards, and as he retold it I could see the vines stir, the wind moving across the long green rows that marched up the slope. I heard the shrieking of cicadas and there were birds with exotic names like beecatcher and shrike that whipped around the eaves. Cats with feral eyes crouched on wide stone ledges next to the blue shutters. It was a dangerous, romantic place. It was called Lanjerow, he said, but then he spelled it: Langoureaux. He paused, as if wanting for me to memorize the spelling.

"A gravity pump fed water from the spring to a stone cistern above the house. It clicked open and shut in a steady rhythm and on hot nights you could hear the beat like a dull metal heart in the vineyard."

As I listened to the words, it seemed like my father was reading from the book. He could not remember the title but could describe the tiniest detail of the stone terrace and an old wrought iron bed half in the shade, half in the blistering sun. His brain had taken all of the energy from his body, he said, and he was being consumed by his thoughts.

"Consumption," he said. "That's what they used to call it. You don't wither away. You get burned up, like a log on a fire, getting smaller and smaller until there's nothing left but white ash."

Such talk frightened me. Larry said not to worry, but I had read my books and I knew he was getting worse. I felt helpless, angry at Metzenbaum, who called me his "little doctor" and smiled while my father was dying.

14

SCHOOL HAD STARTED IN WILLIAMS, twenty miles away, and there was talk of me going to school. The problem was that Dr. Metzenbaum wasn't about to have me driven that distance down the mountain each day. I would have to board with a family in Williams. Nothing much seemed to come of it, and I pretended Mrs. Green was still giving me lessons, sitting in the empty dining room with my books spread on the table looking like I was studying when all I ever did was read and draw pictures. I had come across a book titled *Young Audubon: a Boy's Life in the Caribbean*. He was the son of a French sea captain and it didn't take me long to figure out that Captain Audubon had a wife in France and another one in the West Indies. But what fascinated me was the fact that young Audubon didn't go to school. His father brought him a set of watercolors from France and he spent his days in the fields and swamps, drawing birds. He bought the carcasses of parrots and cockatoos in the markets and propped them up, but they were lifeless and his drawings were just as stiff. He taught himself to stuff the birds. Even these were wooden and he spent his days sketching birds on the wing, coming home each night to his Caribbean mother, his clothes soaked and muddy. He was my age and obsessed with drawing birds, and no adult seemed to mind that he didn't study arithmetic or learn to write a paragraph or read about history. Perhaps I, too, could be like Audubon, learning to draw the birds that flew in the canyons below the sanatorium. But my drawings were as wooden as his first drawings must have been. I was much better at making up stories in which I was the hero, discovering a cure for TB, laboring in my tiny log cabin laboratory in the mountains of Arizona. Or I was arriving in Kentucky in a private railroad car where my mother and my sister waited on the platform in the rain.

I was afraid to broach the subject of school, since it would mean living with strangers and leaving my father at the sanatorium. Finally I asked Larry and he said that no one in Williams would take me because I lived with the lungers.

"They're all afraid of getting it," he said, "When somebody in their family gets TB, they pack them off to places like this and they don't want to know any more about them. You ever notice that nobody comes up here to visit?"

"It's a long way," I said. "Maybe they can't afford to."

"Maybe. But I know one family that put an uncle in a shed behind their house and left his food on the doorstep. It's no good telling them that just because you live here doesn't mean you're contagious. Or that you can be around most lungers and not get it. They don't want to believe it." His voice was angry now and he didn't seem to be talking to me anymore, but to someone else in some other place. "It's not just lungers they're afraid of. They want to shove people like us off into some desert where the wind blows the other direction so they don't have to deal with us."

"Why don't the people in Vallecitos avoid me?"

His voice softened. "Mostly they work here or they know somebody who does and they're Indians who know about TB. Your friend Willie is a Walapai. Most of his people live in shacks along the Santa Fe and there must be a lunger in every house. But they're used to being shunned by the whites. And I don't think they're as afraid of dying as we are."

"Is my father dying?"

"No, Tommy." He ran his hand through my hair. "He's not ever going to die."

"That's not true. Everybody dies."

"Jesus," he said. "You must be about sixty years old."

He took my head in both his hands and bent to look directly at me. "Not for a long time," he said. "I promise you."

I could smell the strong soap the nurses used on his hands.

"Go outside and throw rocks at the blue jays," he said.

15

SOMETIMES IT FELT LIKE the disease was all around me. I felt as if tubercule bacilli were floating around the rooms, drifting in the air. I was sucking them in, invisible red rods that filled each breath.

Tuberculosis was an unwanted guest, a huge man who came, uninvited, to stay with us. He slept in our beds when we were out, ate from our plates and drank from our glasses. No matter how many times he was ordered from the house, he defied us. He was a bum, unshaven and dirty, who sat down at our table. *Go away*, we said, *Get out of here!* But he steadfastly ate, slopping his food down his front, spitting on the floor, hawking and coughing until we could not help but catch whatever it was that he had. He slept with me at night, rolled over snoring and coughing, and when I awoke, drenched with sweat, I was sure I had caught it. I felt my forehead, knew I had a temperature, knew he had come inside me where he squatted on his haunches and picked his nose, flung his snot into the soft pink tissue of my lungs.

I would go out into the dark morning and fill my lungs with sharp air, breathe in and out furiously until my lungs ached and I was light-headed. There was an ice rime on the leaves in the morning now and a thin skin of ice on puddles on the paths. The sides of the cottages remained up, even though the patients could see their breath when they went to bed and there was ice in the bedside drinking glasses in the morning. The nurses brought hot water bottles each evening and my father learned how to make a sausage roll of his bedding so he could slide into the tube with the warm rubber container at his feet.

"I think they're trying to freeze us to death," he joked. He began calling his cottage mates "my fellow Eskimos," and calling Dr. Metzenbaum, "Dr. Shackleton."

September had become October and November approached, three months since we had stepped down from the train at Navajo Junction, but the calendar had a different meaning at Metzenbaum's. In Chicago, days of the week had significance, stores closed on Sunday, there were holidays like the Fourth of July, counting weeks until school started, the Fridays when my father got paid, Sunday picnics; everything seemed marked with a day and a month. Now there was little to distinguish one day from another.

The patients were allowed to get up at seven and they came to the main house to use the bathrooms, with each of the cottages assigned a fifteen-minute period. Breakfast was at eight-thirty, there was time to do light cottage-cleaning chores from nine-thirty until ten, then a required rest in bed until the meal at twelve-fifteen; rest again from one to four with heliotherapy for some. Supper at ten to five. Free time was from six to nine. That was when patients took baths or exchanged books and some were allowed to stroll about the grounds. Supervised crafts took place after supper, consisting of drawing or painting, embroidery, and sometimes weaving braided belts. The shortened days of Fall meant that there were fewer people on the grounds after supper. Lights went on in the cottages, casting little pools of light among the trees.

I don't think my father had planned to stay three months. I knew that I had thought we would come, he would get better, and we would leave, much like going to a hospital for an operation or getting over a bad cold. I, too, was learning to walk instead of run, to speak quietly, drawn into the ever-slowing spiral that seemed to hold patients and staff to a measured cadence, a metronome that wound slowly down.

Several new patients had arrived in those three months and a few had left. Mrs. Green wasn't the only one who had died. My father moved to one of the long walls in the cottage since Bill had left, not cured, but better than when he had first come to the mountain. Henry was still there, but Frank had died. The TB had suddenly galloped through him, he had gone to the main building and, like Mrs. Green, Manuel had taken him down the mountain to be buried at Williams, or to be loaded into a Santa Fe baggage car alongside crates of parts from the Army Supply Depot east of Williams, bound for home. A new man named Jack was in the bed next to the door. No one spoke of the deaths.

I felt as if I would explode. Apparently the plan to leave had withered and died and I was desperate for something to happen. I felt like the cavalry in the Saturday morning westerns, waiting for the Indian attack, watching the silent horizon south of Metzenbaum's mountain, hoping that war cries would fill the air and flaming arrows would suddenly dot the roofs of the cottages. I could not know how soon I would get my wish.

16

THERE ON THE TABLE was a folder marked "examination notes, cottage #4." That was my father's cottage. I stood, looking at the paper folder with the metal hinge. I wanted to open it, see if my father was there; but I knew that to do so would expose me to Dr. Metzenbaum's wrath. Of course, my father's name would be in the folder and I stared at the cover willing it to fall open. Through the window I saw Dr. Metzenbaum striding toward a group of patients sitting in chairs in the sun. I reached down and turned back the cover. Henry's name was on the first sheet. I turned to the second sheet and saw "Edward Hall." Metzenbaum's scrawled handwriting was hard to read, but I managed to make out:

> *high pitched node anterior above 2nd right rib and left*
> *clavicle right apex there are occasional rales increased*
> *by cough pronounced cogwheel breathing harsh*
> *prolonged expiratory sounds breath sounds distant*
> *lower 2/3 of R side p.m. temp 99.6 occas. to 100*
> *from the right hilus up breathing is interrupted*

That was it. I looked out through the window. Metzenbaum was bending over one of the seated patients. They looked like vacationers sunning themselves in their circle of chairs, heads back, cardboard blinders over their eyes, taking their heliotherapy. They might have been in the park on Wacker Drive facing Lake Michigan after a Sunday picnic.

Metzenbaum turned, looked at the building and it seemed he was looking directly at me. I stepped back from the window and scurried to my room. His notes had sounded so mechanical, as if my father's body were filled with cogwheels and valves that ground like gears on a truck or randomly opened and shut, suddenly cutting off his breath. How could his breath sound distant? I got out my old stethoscope from under the mattress and listened to my own breathing, trying to find a cogwheel sound, wondering what a rale was. Was this an ordinary report? Did it say my father was being consumed by his disease? Was his breath more distant because it was fading away and would soon be permanently interrupted? I tried breathing different ways, listening to the sound fade as I softly exhaled, abruptly become a roar in my ears as I sucked in lungfuls of air, but I couldn't find cogwheels, nor could I make the kind of notes I imagined Dr. Metzenbaum was playing on my father's ribs with his steadily tapping fingers.

17

IT SNOWED. "TOO SOON," said Tiny. "Gonna be a long winter. Maybe freeze all of Messinbomb's lungers. " I asked Dr. Metzenbaum what would happen if the winter got so cold that the men and women in the cottages would freeze and he laughed. "Not here," he said. "Who's been filling your head with that?"

When I told him it was one of the Indians, he laughed again. "Lots of superstition there," he said. "It's no wonder they're a dying race." Which struck me as an odd thing for a man to say who was chief of a colony of dying people.

The snow came in the afternoon, slowly at first, thick wet flakes that melted, then stuck to branches and, as it got darker, began to coat everything. Someone was invisibly white-washing the paths, the cottage roofs, the stones that lined the paths. Everything grew enormously silent. I had been reading Robert Louis Stevenson since he, too, was a lunger, and I knew that he had written some things while he was at Saranac, New York, at a famous sanatorium run by a doctor named Trudeau. In the preface to the dog-eared copy of *The Master of Ballantrae*, I found: *I was walking in the verandah of a small cottage outside the hamlet of Saranac. It was winter, the night was very dark, the air clear and cold, and sweet with the purity of forests. For the making of a story here were the conditions, 'Come,' I said to my engine. 'Let us make a tale.'*

Somehow I knew it had been snowing that night at Saranac. I re-read the passage and decided that I, too, would be a writer like

Stevenson. That I would probably get tuberculosis and I would grow to look like him, the lean fragile look that the men and women of Metzenbaum's cottages all had. I would keep a journal of everything that happened at Metzenbaum's and, years from now, when I was dead and everybody I knew was dead, they would be able to see this place. I would be like Mrs. Green, making places come alive with words. When I read Stevenson's words, the page disappeared and I could see the verandah he was walking on, hear his shoes against the wooden floor, even though he made no mention of them. I was transformed into an invisible person, shadowing him, my unseen breath smoking in the cold night air.

It stopped snowing just after lights out and I waited until I was sure everyone was asleep before I dressed and slipped outside. Unlike Stevenson, I had no verandah to walk on and my worn shoes quickly became soaked in the wet snow. My feet felt like lead lumps at the base of my ankles and I kept my arms crossed over my chest with my hands in my armpits. Still, I shivered and it made me think of Chicago and winters with sleds, but this was different. I didn't have my winter jacket and mittens and there were no streetlights, no tracks of cars, no lights from the small dark buildings. The snow seemed luminescent. The light seemed to come from within it.

No smoke came from the cottages. The fires in the square metal stoves in each of the cottages would have burned to embers by now and the patients were not allowed to replenish them. They would be lying in their blanket tubes, soft caps covering their heads, only eyes and noses revealed. By morning there would be ice in the glasses next to their beds. There was no light except for a single yellow window in the main building. The rest of the sanatorium had disappeared. I walked through the snow until I shivered so badly my whole body seemed contorted, and then I went back inside and burrowed deep into my bed. I continued to shiver long after my body had warmed.

The next morning I was out early. Clouds were scudding overhead and the snow was melting. A crow slid across the gray sky and settled on the ridge of a shed, suddenly metallic against the silver wetness of the tin roof. According to Tiny, the crow could work magic. Unlike the magpie, who might be a devil in disguise, the crow wasn't something to be afraid of. He was a scavenger, picking up dead things. Tiny said, "Death isn't anything to be afraid of. It happens all the time." The magpie was something else. Every time Tiny saw one, he touched his forehead and said, "Good morning Mr. Magpie," or "Good afternoon."

"You have to be polite," he said. You never know when one of them is an evil spirit in disguise, just waiting for you to be rude."

When I asked Tiny if he really believed that, he said, "That's what the old people believe. But it don't hurt to say it anyway. Hedge your bet."

There was a raw wind and I had to keep my hands in my pockets to keep them warm. My ears throbbed and my nose was runny. When I reached the cottage, all four men were in bed, blankets up to their chins. The shutters were down and the gloom inside the cottage was broken by four lights, each one fixed to the wall next to a bed. It reminded me of pictures I had seen in *Life* magazine of prisoners of war, Germans, I think, who were being kept in Texas or New Mexico. Without daylight the cottage had lost its openness, had turned into a box with four beds and four lumps of bedclothes with a shadowed face at one end of each lump. I stood in the doorway.

Although it seemed warmer inside, it was only because there was no wind blowing. I could see little puffs of breath above each man's face.

"It's cold," I said. They all turned their faces toward the door. I wiped my running nose on the sleeve of my jacket. "It's Wednesday," I said, feeling somehow that I should explain my appearance in the doorway. My father waved his hand in a circle over his head.

"You look carefully, Tommy, you'll see the Northern lights in here. I believe the polar ice cap is just over there by Henry's bed."

Henry, who had the bed on the northern wall of the cottage, laughed shortly, but the laugh turned into a dry cough that he stifled with a paper handkerchief. He rose on one elbow, reached to the bedside table and picked up a little white paper sputum cup and drooled a blob of spit into it. He carefully replaced the cup and wiped his lips with the handkerchief before lying back.

"Your father is quite the comedian, Thomas. A regular Bob Hope, entertaining us troops here on the Russian Front. I think maybe he should take his show on the road, maybe get a bigger audience."

My father motioned at the chair next to the table.

"Henry was chased by polar bears most of the night, Tommy," he said. "But luckily he escaped by pretending to be a block of ice."

I pulled the chair next to his bed. His face was rosy, the skin on his nose and forehead shining in the dull light, and I could tell that his fever was higher than it had been the last time I visited.

"You're out early. It's not even seven yet."

"It snowed last night," I said. "But it's melting this morning. I was going to get a cardboard box and do some sledding but it's already turned to mush."

"Too bad we didn't bring your sled," he said. Then he added, "Somehow I didn't think of Arizona and snow. All I ever thought about Arizona was sunshine and cactus."

"What's going to happen this winter?" I asked. "Tiny says it's going to be an early winter. Are we going to stay through the snow?"

He leaned toward me and his voice was no more than a whisper. "Do you remember when I said we weren't going to stay here?"

I nodded.

"Well, we're going to leave. We're going to get Larry's car fixed and we're going to Los Angeles. It's all been decided." His voice had a conspiratorial urgency to it, as if it mattered that the others in the tiny cottage not hear; but there was no way they could not know what he was saying.

"I thought maybe you changed your mind," I said.

"No, we have to leave. We haven't enough money to pay Metzenbaum for next month, and besides, I'm not getting any better."

I didn't want to hear this. I wanted to hear him say he was well and we were going back to Chicago where men didn't vomit blood and nobody on our block got put in a coffin in the back of a panel truck.

"What's in Los Angeles?"

"We're going to a place called The City of Hope," he said. "It's one of the best places there is. They can really cure TB. It's in Los Angeles. Or near there."

I could picture this City of Hope, white towers rising at the edge of the Pacific Ocean, long promenades along the sand with wicker wheel chairs being pushed by nurses in starched white. Waves lapped at the sand and the water was brilliant and blue. The towers of the City of Hope glowed in the sun and palm trees marched in stately columns down long avenues. It was, I think, patterned after the city of Oz, from a movie that had made a great impression on me. Mrs. Green's blue men strolled the parapets and the California air was as dry as the desert where nothing could decay, and my father and I would swim in water that would buoy us up in a sea where no one ever drowned. At that moment it was not a fantasy, but a scene as clear in my head as the dim cottage in which I sat with my breath puffing out before me. Why else would a place be named the City of Hope?

"How do you know about it?" I asked.

"Larry knows. He says it's the best place there is for curing lungers. The doctors there know the latest methods. They can collapse an infected lung and give it a rest."

The white towers faded, replaced by the pale green walls of Metzenbaum's isolation room.

"How would you breathe?"

"With the other lung. They'll do something there, Tommy. I can get cured."

"When are we going?" I asked in a rush. I wanted it to be now, this very minute.

"Soon," he said. "But you've got to help."

"Yes!"

"Larry's car needs a new clutch. Do you suppose your Indian friends can fix it?"

I thought of the old car bodies that lay in the yards of Vallecitos like dinosaur skeletons.

"I can ask them. They're always fixing up old cars. Nobody in Vallecitos has a car that runs very good. But if we can't afford to pay Dr. Metzenbaum for next month, how can we afford to go to Los Angeles and the City of Hope?"

"Don't worry about it. Larry has some money saved. And we'll figure out a plan to earn some money when we get to Los Angeles."

I didn't like the sound of that. It wasn't like my father to have plans with contingencies in them. And I wasn't sure how Larry had suddenly become a part of our lives. Why would the money that Larry saved get mixed up with a plan to make my father well? It had been more than three months since the train had deposited the two of us at Navajo Junction and this man had, without my noticing, become a part of us, replacing my absent mother and sister. But he was not my mother, nor was he my father's wife. He wasn't an uncle or someone like Earl Joyner who seemed like a part of the family when he came to our house in Chicago for dinner. Larry had gone from being a nurse caring for my father to the provider of car and money and hope for my father's cure. I did not know whether to be grateful or angry.

18

ALL THAT FALL I HAD spent the long afternoons exploring, hearing sheep baa-ing across the canyons, their cries, guttural bleats and hoarse belches. When the late sun slanted through the trees, the dust kicked up by the sheep filled the spaces between the pines with yellow shifting walls that slid in and out among the trees. They left a hot wooly smell that hung in the air long after the dust had settled and their cries faded down canyon.

After that first snow the sheep were moved off the mountain, bunches of them driven down the road in wooly masses. The woods seemed empty without their cries. Two weeks after the snow, it turned warm again, although the nights remained cold and the mornings found ice on the leaves that now were covering the ground. The gardener raked them against the sides of the cabins and the main building where they would later be covered by winter snow, forming an insulating barrier. I began to range farther and farther down canyon from the sanatorium in my solitary hikes, but after my experience in that first snow, I made sure I was within sight of the sanatorium long before dark.

One afternoon I found myself farther down the canyon than I had ever been. When I started back up, things looked different. I thought I could hear voices far above and worked my way in that direction, but the sound kept shifting, first on one side of me, then the other, then gone altogether. The air turned cold and I wished I had a sweater or jacket. I was alternately hot and sweaty, reaching out to hold onto trees as the slope got steeper, and then cold when I stopped for breath, the rising wind evaporating the sweat. It seemed like I had climbed for a long time, longer than it had taken me to wander down into the canyon, and there was nothing familiar in sight. I stopped and shouted, calling out "Hello!" and waiting. There was no sound of sheep nor an answer, only the rising rush of wind through the trees.

The slope was so steep that I had to crawl on hands and knees and when I turned to look back down, thinking about retreating and trying a different path, I could not see how I had climbed it. I sat, my back at the base of a tree, my heels wedged into the dirt to keep from sliding down, hugging my arms to my chest against the wind. It was getting dark, the sun had moved over the top of the ridge, and I shouted again and again. The only answer was the echo of my voice, mimicking me.

I crawled sideways, working from tree to tree, hoping the slope would somehow diminish. But when I had crawled another thirty yards, the trees opened up and I saw that I was in a box canyon. I had read about box canyons in westerns, but now I saw that it was truly a box, with high layers of red sandstone towering on three sides of me, like Chicago skyscrapers, each level of eroded stone like the separate floor of a building. I could not go forward and I could not retreat. The sun touched the top of the canyon and the layers of sandstone still in the light glowed blood-red and orange. A magpie called from inside the canyon, its shriek echoing vacantly back and forth, making it sound as if it were a flock of magpies. I saw it slip off one of the ledges, slide in a long arc toward me, and pull up, pumping its wings like a man rowing upstream, turning for the other canyon wall where it braked, wings beating as it tried to gain a purchase with its feet, only to fall off and glide effortlessly to the opposite wall. It finally found a perch and yelled at me, or at least it felt like it was yelling at me.

I screamed, "Go to hell!" and then I remembered Tiny's admonition about magpies.

"I'm sorry," I yelled. "I didn't mean it."

I was crying now, certain that God had abandoned us, for I somehow included my father in my predicament, and the haunting hoarse voice on the now-dim ledge had become more than a bird: It was my father's disease, my mother's disappearance, my little sister grown vague, all embroidered in the bird's cry that sporadically echoed in the closeted canyon.

"God damn you!" I yelled. "I don't care!" My anger burst out and I stood, clutching the tree I was braced against. "It's not fair! I didn't do anything!"

I hadn't been a liar or smoked cigarettes or shop-lifted from the dime store like other boys I knew in Chicago. And now my reward was to be lost among sick people, my father lying in bed alternately freezing and burning to death. The City of Hope had been dangled in front of me like some cruel joke.,

"You talk that way to Mr. Magpie and something bad going to happen to you!"

It was Tiny's voce and it came from just above me.

"Help!" I shouted. "I'm down below you."

"I know where you are," he said. "Question is, do you know where you are? Sounds to me like you got yourself in a crack and can't get out." His voice came closer and a cascade of pinecones came down the slope. I watched as he appeared, sliding from tree to tree, his heavy body seemingly out of control; but each tree he passed, he hooked with his arm, swinging in an arc toward the next. He came to a halt ten feet above me.

"How did you know I was here?" I asked, wiping the tears from my streaked face with the sleeve of my shirt.

"Mr. Magpie. Maybe." He paused. "Maybe I just happen to hear you hollering like some calf who just lost his balls. Come on," He reached out his huge hand.

I scrabbled up the slope until I could reach his hand and was suddenly lifted effortlessly alongside him.

"Old deer trail up here," he said, "You almost found it yourself."

He pushed me ahead of him and I crawled, Tiny shoving me until we came to a narrow ledge that wound upwards. The sandstone cliffs were dull red now, the sun below the far ridge. They seemed softer, with clumps of green bush clinging to them. Tiny heaved himself into the trail next to me.

"You got to be careful where you go," he said after he caught his breath. "You ain't no Indian."

"Were you looking for me?"

"That white man nurse who lives in Vallecitos ask me to see if you was in trouble."

"I didn't know anybody knew where I was."

"You be surprised how many people know where you are. Come on. Gonna be dark. Freeze our nuts." He rose and shambled bear-like up the narrow trail.

"You won't tell anybody what happened to me, will you?"

"I keep to myself," he said. "It's safer that way."

On the steeper parts I reached ahead and hooked my hand into his belt, towed along, I'm sure, with no more weight than a minor nuisance to the big man. He rolled from side to side as he climbed, head bent forward on the upslope with an agility surprising for his size. There was no more talk. When we broke out onto the top, it was dark enough that the ground was barely visible.

"You go straight there," he said, pointing to a gap in the trees ahead. "You see the lights of Messinbombs. You'll be okay now," and he went off to the right toward the Vallecitos road.

"Thanks, " I called after him, but there was no answer. I decided that I would make Tiny the hero of my journal about Metzenbaum's. I tried to imagine him astride a barrel-chested horse, dressed in feathers and hides. The cavalry would have no chance against a foe like that. Maybe I would have to branch out and write stories about the West in which Indians won the battles.

I shuffled along in the dark, feeling with my feet for rocks or holes. At the gap in the trees, the lights of the sanatorium showed, leaving a long streak on the ground, like a pathway leading to safety.

I remembered walking to Arlington Park when my sister was six and I was eight. That summer we lived in a rented house in Arlington Heights. It was late in the Fall when the racing season had closed and we set out to see the racetrack. My father was working at Oak Park where the trotters ran until it snowed and we had wrapped cheese sandwiches in wax paper and left the house, finally leaving the streets behind and crossing the last fields around the racetrack that belonged to a farmer who had not sold out to the encroaching city.

The ground was rough, clods of sticky dirt turned over, bits of sharp corn stubble turned in all directions. It was hard to follow the furrows and our low-cut shoes were soon scratched and muddy, my sister's legs streaked with red where the stubble had raked her. By the time we got to the racetrack, long shadows stretched across the infield and the sun was a dull orange ball in the hazy light. We ate our sandwiches in the cavernous grandstand but we didn't play. The lateness of the hour and the emptiness of the place frightened us and we set out for home. My sister was tired and complained that she couldn't walk. I kept telling her it was only a block away, but I could see across the long fields that the houses were still far off. There was a white rime on the stubble, frost setting in, and our breath showed in the failing light. Then the lights went on in the low row of houses at the far end of the field and we could sense the warmth in those houses. We began to run, falling and slipping, our hands coated with mud, both of us crying and breathing hard until we came to the first street and the street lights that told us home was close.

My father was angry with me for taking her and angry that we had gone so far but my mother asked if it had been an adventure and wanted to know what we had seen. She opened a can and heated tomato soup that burned in my throat.

The lights of Metzenbaum's were closer now and I wondered what my sister was doing, what she looked like now, and where she and my mother were. Metzenbaum's was not home—it was a place to be while my father got well. I wanted that to happen tomorrow.

19

LARRY'S CAR WAS GUN-METAL GRAY, a sedan of immense proportions with long fenders that curved down to running boards on both sides and a bulbous trunk on the back. The hood was long and narrow and the inside of the car was narrow as well, belying the fact that the car had a battleship-like appearance.

Tiny took a wrench from a battered metal fishing tackle box and crawled under the car. After a half hour of cursing and clanking, he crawled out.

"It's as tight is it's gonna get," he said, and we climbed in, Willie in the driver's seat, the Chief next to him, and Tiny and me in the back seat. The car lurched when Willie cranked it over.

"Ain't going to start this way," Willie said. "No way at all." Tiny and the Chief got out, went to the rear of the car, squatted and turned their backs to the trunk, lifting with their hands on the bumper. They pushed that way, grunting, while the car inched forward, picking up speed down the hill, coughing, the motor trying to catch in compression. Tiny had tightened the clutch so much that the engine was engaged even when the clutch pedal was depressed.

There was a wrenching sound of gears clashing as Willie shifted and the motor coughed and jerked while Tiny and the Chief ran to leap onto the running boards and climb in. The motor came to life and the Olds picked up speed.

"Hot damn!" Willie shouted, cranking open the windshield so that air began to flood into the car. I clutched the ten-dollar bill my father had given me in my fist inside my pocket. We flew down the mountain, dust filling the car, Willie riding the brake until the smell of burning brake pads nearly overpowered us. Then the road flattened out, we bounced across the tracks at Navajo Junction, and five miles later we turned onto the main road to Williams.

It took an hour to get to Williams, despite the fact that it was only fifteen miles. No matter how tight Tiny had fastened the clutch, it continued to slip, and by the time we came past the first brick buildings that announced the edge of town, the car could do no more than three or four miles an hour, the engine racing. We went past the Fray Marcos Hotel and the Santa Fe depot, turned across the tracks and rolled past a run-down house surrounded by old car bodies, junked logging equipment, pieces of boilers, and a faded boxcar without wheels.

Willie turned off the motor but it continued to fire, so hot it needed no spark to ignite the gas, and Tiny opened the flap on the side of the hood, smothering the top of the carburetor with his bandana until the motor choked to a halt.

A man came to the door of the boxcar, wiping his hands on a rag. He stood there silently.

"We're looking for a clutch plate," Tiny said.

"That your car?" the man asked, mouth hardly moving at all.

"No," Tiny said. "It belongs to this kid's father who works at Messinbombs and he hired us to fix it."

I held up the crumpled ten-dollar bill.

"You find what you need," the man said. "And don't take nothing else." He went back inside the darkness of the boxcar.

"Piss on you," Tiny muttered and the three of them began to poke among the car bodies. It took an hour to find a clutch plate that would fit and still another hour before they had the transmission pulled loose and the plate bolted on.

It was beginning to get dark and a light was on in the house when we assembled at the door. The three of them held back while I knocked. The man came and stood in the rectangle of light.

"What you get?" he asked.

"We got the plate outta a '37 Chevy," Tiny said.

"How the hell you red niggers make that fit?" the man asked.

"Wasn't easy," Tiny said, his voice even, as if he had not heard the last words.

"Five dollars," the man said. I held out the ten-dollar bill.

"Shit," he said. "I thought you had a five."

He went inside and came back with a five-dollar bill. "What you doing with them?" he said to me.

"My father sent me with the money."

"Smart man. They woulda drunk it all up by now." He turned and the door closed.

We got back into the car without speaking. It took a while for the motor to catch, but when Willie let out the clutch pedal, the car moved forward smoothly. We bumped over the tracks and stopped in the wide gravel lot behind the Fray Marcos Hotel. A Santa Fe switch engine rumbled on a siding, the ground vibrating in tune with the thump of the steam cylinders.

"How about you go inside and get us some beers," Willie said to me.

"They won't sell it to me," I said.

"He's right," Tiny said. "How about you give us three of those dollars so we can get us a drink. Come on, Tommy, nobody's gonna know, and that five you got is for us fixing this thing anyway, right?"

I didn't know what to say. `

"We'll be right back," the Chief said. "We ain't gonna drink it here. We'll get us a bottle and take us all back to Vallecitos first, okay?"

Reluctantly I held out the five-dollar bill. My father hadn't said anything about giving it to them. I started to get out but Tiny said, "No, Somebody got to watch the car. You stay here." And they were gone, disappearing past the hotel, then reappearing as they crossed the tracks toward the line of brick buildings on the opposite side. They didn't come back right away. I waited while the switch engine went off; it became dark and I fell asleep curled up against the edge of the back seat, the roof of the car faintly lit by the street lights across the track.

There was a thumping at the car and I sat bolt upright. Outside were two figures carrying what appeared to be a third. Willie opened the back door and in the faint light I could see that Tiny was on the ground, his head and shoulders held up by the Chief. Willie got into the back seat and I scrunched over to the far side. He turned and helped drag Tiny's body to the edge of the car. Together they got him into the back seat, half on the seat and half off. His face was covered with blackened blood, and his eyes were swollen shut. One ear hung down at a funny angle. It took a few seconds for me to realize that it was nearly torn off.

We drove back to Vallecitos in silence, broken only by an occasional gurgling from Tiny, his head cradled on the Chief's lap.

I sat in front while Willie drove, both hands tight to the wheel, his eyes intent on the road ahead. We were almost to the turn off to Navajo Junction when I asked, "What happened to Tiny?"

Willie didn't take his eyes off the road. "We went to the back door of the Grand Canyon Club and asked if we could buy a bottle. We had us a couple of drinks there in the alley, but some cowboy heard us and came out and said no prairie niggers was allowed there. Tiny said, 'That's the second time today I hear that word,' and the cowboy said 'What word?' and Tiny said, 'You oughtta know, General Custer,' and the guy went back in and came out with a half dozen of them. They was all drunked up and they beat Tiny something awful. Wasn't nothing we could do. They would of killed all three of us. They used a pool cue on him. He banged them up some before he went down."

We raced across the flats toward the mountains. A jackrabbit, startled in the headlights, froze, and there was a thump as the car hit him.

"Bad night for everyone," Willie said. There was no noise except the grinding of the motor as we climbed through the dark firs to Vallecitos. They stopped at the little house where Tiny lived with his grandmother and carried him inside. Then Willie drove the car to Larry's house across the ravine where he talked with him and Larry made a bed for me on the couch. I felt numb and asked him if Tiny would be all right, but he said go to sleep, Sport, and sat on the edge of the couch stroking my forehead until I slept.

The next morning I wanted to see how Tiny was, but Larry said I should go back with him to the sanatorium since they would be worried about me. He made breakfast, oatmeal and hot chocolate, and we left his little house across the ravine from the Indian houses and drove in the Oldsmobile to Metzenbaum's.

Everything seemed to be the same, although after the events of the night before, I expected them to look different. The dark firs still lined the road and patches of frost left the pine needles on the edge of the road looking like they'd been dusted with flour.

"They did a good job," Larry said as he shifted the Olds into low gear for the last ascent to the sanatorium. I had forgotten about the clutch.

He took me directly to my father's cottage where the men were up in their bathrobes, all except for my father who was fully dressed. They were gathering their toilet articles and towels for the morning trip to the washroom in the main building.

My father listened intently as Larry explained what had happened. Apparently Willie had told him most of the night's events, and when he finished my father asked if I was all right.

"Yes," I said. "Will Tiny be all right?"

"He got beat up pretty badly," Larry said. "They had to get Metzenbaum down to tend to him." That part surprised me since I couldn't imagine Dr. Metzenbaum mending cuts or broken limbs or sewing back a ripped ear. He had been a thumper and listener, not a real doctor.

"The car runs fine, Eddie," Larry said.

My father nodded. "You're sure you're all right?" he asked again.

"Can I go back to Vallecitos this afternoon and see Tiny?"

"No. You stay here. I want you to stick close. Larry will find out and let you know first thing tomorrow."

"When are we going to California?" I asked. I wanted desperately to be someplace where Indians were part of books and nobody called them prairie niggers and people didn't take their temperature three times a day and I could run until I was exhausted and nobody would tell me to stop. I was tired of being a leper's child and having lepers for friends.

"Soon," he said, and I could see the other three men pretending they weren't listening.

I spent the rest of the day hanging around the kitchen watching Manuel work. He knew about Tiny's beating, as did everyone who came from Vallecitos, and he cursed in English and Spanish: "Goddammed cucarachas ought to get their cojones cut off."

After lunch, Dr. Metzenbaum found me and took me aside.

"I don't know what you were doing in Williams with those men, but you could have been hurt very badly. I've told your father that I can't be responsible for you if you keep company with men like that."

"They're very nice," I protested.

"They may seem very nice to a twelve-year-old, but they lead the kind of lives that no twelve-year-old should be exposed to, and you need to exercise some judgment. I don't know why I ever agreed to having you here with your father."

He took a deep breath and stuck his hands deeper into the pockets of his white doctor's coat. A little row of thermometers and pencils and pens of different colors lined the top pocket.

"Your father says he doesn't have an address for your mother. I don't suppose you would have one." It wasn't a question, but more of a statement of fact made in the air above my head. I wasn't sure if I was supposed to say anything.

"Good Lord," he finally said, still looking over the top of my head.

"Will Tiny be all right?"

"No, I don't think your friend will make it. I've never seen a body that took so much punishment, unless it was in the war." It took me a few seconds to realize that he was not talking about the war that was just ending, but he was talking about the First World War and I wondered if this large soft man had fought in that war.

"You're not as tough a little nut as you pretend to be," he said. "Some day all of this pus is going to come to a head and somebody is going to have to lance it. I'm sorry about your friend. I'm sure he was a good person."

"Manuel," he said to the cook. "Keep an eye on Tommy. Maybe you've got a treat of some kind he can have."

"*Si,*" Manuel replied, banging pots as he cleared away the counter. "*Yo puedo cuidado. Es un buen muchacho.*"

I went to bed early, read for a while and then, after I turned out the light, I lay in bed shaking, although the room was warm. The back seat of the Oldsmobile in the darkness came to me, and Tiny's smashed dark face, so I turned the light back on and went to sleep with the brightness of the lamp outlining the veins in my closed eyelids.

20

I KEPT OUT OF everyone's way the next day, but I went to my father's cottage three times. We didn't talk much. I just stood outside the screen on his side of the cottage for a few minutes each time, wanting to ask him when we were leaving and knowing that he would tell me when the time came. That we were going to leave was now a fact—it was just a matter of when.

Larry didn't come to work, so I didn't know how Tiny was, but Dr. Metzenbaum's words the day before left me feeling that I didn't want to know.

Willie came to the Sanatorium late in the afternoon and found me in the kitchen again with Manuel.

"Tiny's dead," he said. "You come to Vallecitos tonight."

Manuel started to protest. "He's not going no place, hombre," but Willie ignored him.

"Chief says you should be there. We're going to burn his house."

"Why?"

"Tiny was White River Apache. His old people believe that when someone dies they should burn the teepee."

"He didn't live in no teepee," Manuel said. "He lived in a goddammed house. What you want to do that for? What the hell you gonna do with the old grandmother?"

"Don't give me any crap, Manny. Chief says we should do this because Tiny would want us to. I don't care either way. But Chief says the kid was with us that night and he should be there when we do it."

"You leave Tommy out of this," Manuel insisted. "What you rojos do is your own business, but you shouldn't mix him in it. He's had enough grief already."

"Nobody's gonna get hurt," Willie said. "You be there when it's dark, okay? Just after sundown. And you," he turned to Manuel, "you keep your nose out of this."

"*Ve te al infiermo*," muttered Manuel and he turned his back on Willie.

Manuel didn't try to stop me, nor did he tell anyone where I was going that evening. I ate in the kitchen with him and went back to my room, turned the light on before closing the door, and slipped out the back of the building.

I hurried along the darkening road, my heart pounding and my nose and ears so cold that my head ached. I found Willie and the Chief in front of Tiny's house.

"As soon as this is over you go right back to Messinbombs," the Chief said. "We never did anything like this before and I don't want nothing bad to happen to you. I just felt like you should be here when we did this because you was there in Williams that night, and besides he used to say you talked to magpies. I don't know what any of that shit means, but him dying this way is like a seam unraveling and we got to stitch it up again. You stay here."

He and Willie went into the darkened house and a few minutes later came out with a short, squat woman built like a fireplug, wearing a faded dress whose hem dragged on the ground. The Chief on one side and Willie on the other had a hand under each armpit, and they moved impassively across the bare earth to the next house where a woman waited, several children gathered like curious night animals. The old woman looked straight ahead as if she were looking at some far distant thing that did not move. This was Tiny's grandmother and the house had been hers. Two rooms with a tin roof; it was like any other Indian house in Vallecitos.

The woman in the doorway took one arm of the old woman and the Chief came back. He picked up a five-gallon can and went into the empty house. A minute later he came out and walked around the house, sloshing the contents on the weathered boards. The smell of kerosene filled the night air. Finally he threw the empty can through the doorway.

"You better get back," he said to me. The children had reappeared in the doorway of the house next door and Willie came out, holding a blanket.

The chief struck a match and tossed it at the kerosene-soaked wall. It went out in midair and he lit another, touched it to the box of matches and, when the box flared, threw the whole thing. There was a pause, then a soft sucking sound as flame leaped up the wall, spread sideways, lapping at the eaves. Within seconds the house was enveloped. There was a roar as the inside caught and a column of fire rose into the still blackness. The smell of kerosene was intense and my face was so hot it felt as if my skin were on fire. I turned to retreat. People stood behind me silently in knots along the street. When they had appeared I did not know, but there was no talk, only the shiny flat faces reflecting the flames. When I turned back to the fire, orange embers were rising and there were whirling leaves and bits of grass being sucked into the vortex like moths entering the flame.

The walls were burnt out before the supporting timbers collapsed, and I could see a table and a chair weirdly afire before the twisted tin roof dropped into the crackling pile of burning timbers and boards. It seemed like only a few minutes before the house was reduced to a smoking pile of trash, and the people who had lined the street disappeared as silently as they had appeared.

Now that the fire was gone it was suddenly cold. My eyes watered and when I wiped my nose on my sleeve, it smelled of smoke and kerosene. I was glad when Larry appeared. We walked to where his Olds was parked.

"What happened to your motorcycle?" I asked.

"Sold it. Sold my Indian to some Indians." On the way back to the Sanatorium he asked who had told me about the burning of Tiny's house. When I told him Willie had come to Metzenbaum's to tell me to be there, he said I had seen something special and that I would probably only understand it when I was away from this place. Tomorrow we would leave for California or bust. He laughed and said maybe we should paint that on the side of the car.

"It's too bad Willie and the Chief can't come with us."

"Why is that?"

"They could get parts in movies. They look more like Indians than the ones I used to see in the movies."

"Surprise," Larry said. "We're giving them a ride to the coast. I need somebody to keep our Conestoga wagon running." He thumped the steering wheel with the heel of his hand.

"Are they going to live with us?"

"Jesus, no. They're the last thing I need."

"You like them, don't you?"

"Sure, Tommy. But they're not going to sit still in one place very long. God forbid if they ever did get parts in a movie; they'd probably load their rifles with real bullets and kill a few fake cavalrymen."

"They wouldn't kill anybody!"

"No, you're right. But I sure wouldn't want to be some fat actor who had to tell Willie, 'Me trade you wampum for your squaw.'" He thumped the wheel of the Olds again. "California or bust," he repeated. "Make us a sign to stick on the back of the car, will you, Sport?"

Larry brought the Olds to Metzenbaum's the next morning and my father and I put our suitcase into the trunk. I had a box of books that Dr. Metzenbaum said I could keep and Larry taped my carefully lettered sign just below the back window. Dr. Metzenbaum wished my father good luck and told him he should get treatment as soon as he got to Los Angeles, not to wait, that every day counted. Everybody shook hands and Dr. Metzenbaum told Larry he would miss him, that he was a good nurse and would be hard to replace. He pressed Larry's hand between his two soft hands and held them for a moment longer and said he hoped California would be kind to us.

Then we were off, down the road to Vallecitos where Willie and the Chief were waiting for us on the porch of the store. They each had a cloth sack with their stuff in it that they squashed into the trunk, but it wouldn't entirely close and they had to use a piece of rope to tie the handle to the bumper. Willie put a stained cloth waterbag on one of the headlights so that it hung down in the little valley between the fender and the hood, and then the two of them squeezed into the back seat, one on either side of me. We were on the move again, this time with a man who wore a silver dinosaur pin and two Indians who wanted to become movie stars.

CALIFORNIA

21

WE CAME DOWN FROM San Bernardino into Los Angeles and kept right on driving until we came to Santa Monica and the ocean. Larry parked the car in the parking lot off a little café. The sidewall was a painted sign that advertised hot dogs and hamburgers and Mexicali beer for 35 cents a pitcher. We took off our shoes and walked through the hot sand to the edge of the ocean. Larry waded out and turned to us.

"Come on, Eddie! Come on, Tommy! Get your feet wet. It's the Pacific Ocean, for God's sake!"

My father began to roll up his trouser legs, but Larry splashed out of the water and grabbed him by the arm, towing him back into the shallow surf until their trousers were wet to the knees. I ran in after them and stood as the waves came in, feeling the sand running out from under my toes as each wave receded. The Chief and Willie stood at the edge of the parking lot, watching us.

The horizon seemed endless. I had grown used to long vistas in Arizona, but this was something else. In front of me was nothing but blue-green water as far as I could see. I had reached the edge of the continent.

We went looking for a place to stay. Willie and the Chief took their cloth bags and said goodbye. They took the Pacific Electric trolley car back into Los Angeles where they had a friend they said would put them up. Although I knew that they were young men, it wasn't until we were far away from Vallecitos that they lost some of their bravado, and I realized they were not that much older than I was. I had thought of them as men, but Willie was only seventeen and the chief was nineteen. Tiny had been the oldest at twenty-three. Now, a thousand miles from the mesa, and with Tiny gone, the other two seemed smaller, less like my romantic view of Indians and more like two out-of-place boys in the flatlands of Los Angeles. There was no mention of the movies. There were other Indians who had come to Los Angeles, they said, and like them, they would find work in the shipyards or in the oil fields. If worse came to worse, they could always pick oranges.

We found a house on Ocean Avenue with an "apartment for rent" sign. An old man showed us two connected rooms with a tiny bathroom under the eaves, the slanted ceiling so low that you had to back into the toilet. The smaller room was a bedroom. In the corner of the larger room was a sink and a shelf with a hot plate. An ancient refrigerator with a cooling coil on top stood behind a small partition. Larry and my father would sleep in the little bedroom. I would have the cot in the living room-kitchen. Things were falling into place.

The next morning I awoke to sun and the ocean, spread out blue on the opposite side of the street. There was a faint smell of oil in the air and at the end of the block an oil pump dipped and rose, dipped and rose like a prehistoric animal whose mouth had been fixed to the earth with a metal rod. The muffled throb of the engine that powered it was softer than it had been at night, mixed with the thump of waves and the early morning traffic on Ocean Avenue.

I said nothing about going to school and my father was content to let me alone. He was weak from the trip and spent most of the day on the threadbare couch in the window facing the ocean, the curtains open. "Heliotherapy," he joked. "Metzenbaum would be proud of me."

Larry was off immediately after breakfast in search of a job and the second morning he announced that he had found work as a cook at Spencers Snack Shop and had sold the Oldsmobile. Trolley cars seemed to run everywhere, down the center of Ocean Avenue in front of our apartment, south to Long Beach and Huntington Park, and east beyond Los Angeles all the way to San Bernardino. They were all colors, some of them red, some yellow, others green and yellow.

There was no need for a car, he said, and he had gotten a hundred dollars for it from two sailors who were headed home. Besides, gasoline and tires were scarce and where would we want to go that the Big Red Cars wouldn't take us.

"Two absolutely pathetic gobs were in Spencers complaining that they couldn't find a ride to Nebraska, and I said, 'Hello, sailors, have I got a deal for you,' and before you could say abracadabra, I separated them from this." He fanned out twenty-dollar bills the same way Earl Joyner had fanned out cards in our living room in Chicago.

The phrase, "Hello sailors," was said with the word 'hello' drawn out in a lilting dramatic voice that seemed so funny I laughed out loud, but my father only frowned and shook his head, as if he disapproved of what Larry had done.

Larry laid the fan of bills on the table. "We're on our way," he said. "Come on, Eddie, lighten up." He winked at me. At that moment I liked him enormously. Only good things could happen from now on.

The beach during the week was deserted and I raced along it that first morning, running in and out of the water. A policeman shouted at me and when I came up to the edge of the street he demanded to know why I wasn't in school.

"I'm just visiting," I said. "I'm here to see my father who has TB and is at the City of Hope and my mother went to see him. My aunt lives there." I pointed to the building on the corner.

I was surprised how easily the lie had come to me. The next day when he saw me on the beach, he waved. I waved back.

That first week I watched some men pulling homemade scoops through the sand, looking for things lost by sunbathers. The scoops were wooden, shaped like a big dustpan with a piece of screen on the back, and when they were pulled, the lip scooped up the top two or three inches of sand. It spilled out through the screen, leaving bits of wood, shells, and occasionally quarters and nickels trapped by the screen. There were two men who worked the Santa Monica beach, solemnly pulling in long rows where the umbrellas had crowded the sand on Sunday, stopping periodically to empty the box of trash, sifting through for anything valuable.

I made a scoop of my own, using wood from crates I found at the back of a grocery store, pounding the old nails flat with a rock and using a piece of screen I cut from a sash I found in the basement of the apartment house. It wasn't as efficient as the ones the beach men had, and I had to stop every ten feet to empty it since the mesh of my screen was far too fine. I did my searching in the early morning, before the two men got to the beach, and by Friday I had nearly three dollars in change.

The second week my father said I had to go to school. On Monday morning we walked together to the grade school that was nearest to us and I was enrolled. My father signed all the right papers and I was led off to a sixth-grade classroom. I knew immediately I was too old for sixth grade, that I should have been in junior high school, but the teacher was a nice older woman who gave me a desk in the back of the room and introduced me to the class as a "new boy from Arizona. Perhaps we can learn all about the Grand Canyon from him." I lasted three days. On Thursday I left the house just as if I were going to school, but I stopped at a little café near the pier and used the pay phone in the back next to the men's room to call the school and tell them we were moving back to Arizona.

"My father has tuberculosis," I said. "He's going to a sanatorium near Phoenix and I'm going to live with my mother in Kentucky." The school secretary asked if she could speak to my father, but I told her he had gone to Union Station to get train tickets. He would call her later if he could. We just wanted to thank them for accepting me and hoped I hadn't been too much trouble.

It was the tuberculosis part that put her off. And, of course, we had no phone, so nobody could call back. I crossed my fingers that no truant officer would appear at the apartment.

The war was over and servicemen, mostly sailors, crowded the towns along the coast. They stood on corners, gathered in parks, and strolled the nearly empty amusement parks that were at the end of huge piers from Santa Monica to Huntington Beach. The big rides and the ballrooms were closed during the week, but on weekends they came alive and the beaches were crowded with umbrellas, the trolleys jammed with people carrying blankets and folding chairs and radios and beach balls. I couldn't get over the idea that winter was approaching in Chicago, but here people were swarming to the beach where the temperature on some days rose as high as eighty degrees.

22

WE MOVED AGAIN to a house in Venice, right on the ocean. It was one of a row of ramshackle wooden houses leaning crazily toward each other with a wooden sidewalk and a dirt strip and then railroad tracks. Beyond that was the beach, not like the fashionable beach at Santa Monica, but oil-splotched with a sour smell. My father walked on the beach now and seemed to be better. He still spit into paper cups, as if he expected a nurse to collect them so the contents could be examined, but of course there was no nurse to collect them. Each afternoon he took them into the backyard and burned them in the incinerator, an old oil drum with the top cut off and holes cut around the bottom edge for draft. He threw wadded-up newspaper in, and when it was burning fiercely, he dropped the cups in and waited until it had all turned to ash. He was looking each time to see if there was blood mixed in with the stuff he coughed up, a sign that he had open lesions in his lungs.

We went through the ritual of enrolling me in school again. I had a moment of panic in the school office when they asked the name of the school I had gone to and my father turned to me. For an instant I couldn't remember the name, and I said, "I'm sorry. I wasn't paying attention. What was the question?" The second time I remembered.

They put me in seventh grade this time, but by the end of the week I knew I wasn't going to stick it out. I had already taken an afternoon off to explore the canals that snaked through Venice. On Friday, I telephoned the school and told them that we were moving back to Arizona so my father could get treatment for his TB. I was on the loose again.

That night Larry and my father told me they had been to the City of Hope. I had given up on this mythical place, but sure enough, it existed and they had been there. It was in Arcadia, east of Los Angeles, and my father said it cost $12.50 a day. There were lots of Jews there, and some people called it the "Jewish Hospital," but that was okay, they took others, too. His name was on a waiting list. It had been called the Los Angeles Sanatorium, and it took in charity cases from Los Angeles, but you had to be a resident to get charity and we hadn't been there long enough.

"What about you?" I asked Larry.

He looked at my father, then at me.

"What about me? " he said.

"Don't you have TB, too?"

He looked again at my father. "What did you tell him?" he asked.

"That you tested positive."

"When?"

"At Metzenbaum's."

He turned to me. "Tommy, I don't have TB. I tested positive, but that happens to a lot of nurses who work in sans. I got checked the first week we got here and there's no sign I'm infected. Your father should have told you." He turned to my father. "We should get him x-rayed, too. Christ, do I have to do everything? Why in the hell did I get mixed up with you two?

There was a long silence. I wanted to say something, but I had no idea what to say. The air had been sucked out of the room, and even if I said something, no sound would come out of my mouth. Larry spoke again.

"I'm sorry, Eddie. It's just that I'm so damn tired. It's not much fun, is it?" He turned to me. "There's a public health clinic in Los Angeles where you can get your x-ray. Eddie will give you a note. You can get there on the Red Car. You ought to be able to figure out the Red Cars. You're a clever kid and I'm sure you won't mind missing a day of school."

The way he said it told me immediately that he had either guessed what I was doing or knew about it.

"Maybe Sunday we'll have a picnic on the beach," he said. "What do you say? Tommy can bring his scoop and find me a diamond ring. Okay, Sport?"

Sure I said. Somehow, I knew, I would have to find a way to get back into school.

But my resolve had melted by Monday morning. I rode the Red Car into Los Angeles for my x-ray and it opened up another world for me. I knew I couldn't hang around the beach since my father might spot me, so I began riding the Red Cars, the big trolleys that ran up and down the coast and east into Los Angles in a giant web of electric lines, using the money I found on the beach. They were powerful things, dull red with an orange stripe around the top. The motorman stood in the center of the front window, his hand on an iron lever that turned out to be a portable wrench he took with him whenever he left the car. He stood there in khaki pants and shirt, a black bowtie and a hat with a shiny bill, staring straight ahead as the tracks rushed beneath us, slowly down the coast on Ocean Avenue, but faster, nearly sixty miles an hour on the express that sped east toward Los Angeles.

I could board the car, pay my fare, and get a transfer and ride for hours, going south to Redondo Beach, transferring east to Watts, then north again toward downtown, straight at the mountains that loomed beyond LA, only to go west at Valley Junction toward the coast, riding all the way to Santa Monica. Sometimes I started north, then followed the tracks as they went through Soldiers Home, Beverly Hills, and Hollywood, hoping to catch a glimpse of a movie star, something that never happened, looping down again to the central terminal in Los Angeles. Once I spent the day going east on the long line that stretched nearly sixty miles to San Bernardino, The problem was that I had to buy a new ticket back and it was far more expensive than going up and down the coast.

I looped in long circles and figure eights for hours, and each motorman assumed I was a kid who was going someplace, to a relative or an appointment. It was the perfect world for a kid cutting school. The cars rocked along past orange groves, shiny green trees with splotches of bright orange, ladders thrust into them and brown-skinned people clustered around trucks piled high with crates. Sometimes there were fields of strawberries, workers bent over the dense green rows, and in Venice I sped along canals where white swans glided on still water that was brownish green and lapped at the edges of stuccoed bungalows. In Long Beach we circled Signal Hill, a forest of oil derricks that looked as if some giant child had skinned off the rolling slopes to build with the world's biggest erector set. The air there was always filled with the stench of burning oil and sulfur and the people looked burnt as well. Men in blackened overalls with grease-stained caps would board the car and sit next to me, and I could smell the oil on them and wondered if the sandwiches in their tin lunch boxes tasted of oil as well.

Most of them spoke with a southern accent, but it was a hard sound, full of twanging and cursing. They seemed like hard men and they came from Oklahoma and Texas and Arkansas, but they were friendly, always said, "How you doing, sonny?" when they slid into the wicker seat next to me, asking where I was going or what I was doing, as if they had to check up on a kid out of school on a weekday. That was how I met Bunny.

Bunny Smith came from Oklahoma and his father was a rigger for Shell on Signal Hill. I found out that meant he worked on the drilling derricks, coupling pipes together with wrenches as big as my leg. Charlie Smith was a wiry man who didn't look big enough to do that sort of work, but he was strong, and the first time I met him he said, "I've got a kid about your age and if you're anything like him, you ain't going to see your aunt like you say—you just don't want to go to school," and he gave me a wink that squeezed the whole side of his leathery face.

It was nearly noon, and we were riding north away from Signal Hill toward downtown.

"No sir, my aunt lives in Compton." It was a stop farther up the line from Long Beach.

"I live at Willowbrook," he said, and I realized it was three stops past Compton. I would have to get off the car and board another one.

"Actually, I'm not getting off at Compton," I said. "I'm meeting her in Watts and we're going to my cousin's house in Redondo Beach. She works downtown," I added, hoping that would explain why she would be at a station north of where she lived.

"Well," he said, looking past me out the window. "I got an aunt like that, too. She's a mighty handy aunt. But if you'd like to disappoint her and get off at Willowbrook with me, you can have dinner with us." I had not heard the midday meal referred to as "dinner" since I had left Illinois.

So I got off the car at Willowbrook and ate with the Smiths. Bunny was there, for his school was only five blocks away and he always ate at home. Mrs. Smith had the meal ready when we came through the door. She didn't seem surprised to see me, as if bringing home a stray kid was something her husband might often do. There was a sister, a carbon copy of her mother in a dress that looked as if it had been made out of the same material as her mother's, and there was much laughter.

"This here's Tom," Mr. Smith said. "I have rescued him from the clutches of an unreliable aunt who may or may not live somewhere between Compton and the San Gabriel mountains. He looked hungry."

Nobody said anything about why I wasn't in school, and after we ate pork chops and mashed potatoes covered with a thick white gravy, I walked back to Bunny's school with him.

"I'd ride to your house," he said, "but my dad gave me a whipping for not being in school last Friday." We stood outside the school until the bell rang. He promised that he would meet me in front of Duke's Corn-on-the-Cob at Ocean Park Pier on Saturday, and then he joined the throng of noisy kids going into the low brick building.

I thought again about going to school. I had always liked school, the neatness of it and the order of things, the dependable cycle of spelling and reading and arithmetic and geography and maps and dodgeball. It was something I did well. I think I had become afraid of school. Perhaps it was because I had not gone to school for more than five months, but something else was at work. I was, consciously or otherwise, trying to be less of a good boy, withdrawing from the sick man in the small house who was my father, distancing myself from his illness. Perhaps the further I got from him, the better his chances for recovery.

If my father knew I was cutting school, he didn't let on. I think he was glad I spent so little time in the house. I suppose he thought it would lessen the chance of me contracting TB, but I had had so much contact with him over the past year that it probably didn't make much difference.

He asked me what was going on in school, and I made up things to tell him: countries we studied, books we had to read. I pretended to go over spelling lists, repeating the words out loud and making them into sentences, hoping it would convince him I was going to school, but it seemed like an elaborate charade that neither of us was willing to acknowledge. He did not know what to do with me and I was busy trying not to think about him. I missed the Wednesday afternoons by the little cottage at Metzenbaum's where I was convinced that he would get well. There had been a regimen to our lives there, a regularity that could be counted on. Here, everything seemed random, the sun shone bright on beach umbrellas in November and you could pick oranges off a tree that hung over the sidewalk not twenty yards from our house. I rode in circles most days, waiting for Bunny to get out of school.

Larry seemed oblivious. He left early for work, came home late, worked Friday nights at the Egyptian Ballroom at the end of Ocean Park Pier, and had a cleaning job Saturday at the Cooper Arms, a six-story apartment building in Santa Monica. It was a fancy, L-shaped building with high arched windows on the ground floor, elaborate wrought-iron fire escapes, and stubby palm trees that lined the street separating it from the beach. Next door were the Terry Apartments and next to that was an old house with a glassed-in front porch and a second attic floor with two windows overlooking the ocean. A faded sign said "BEACH HOTEL" across the front, but it no longer took in guests.

We moved again, this time to the second floor of Mrs. Evola's defunct beach hotel in Santa Monica because it was cheaper than the house in Venice. Our rooms no longer shook from the long trains of oil cars that passed in the night. The rooms had sharply slanted ceilings so that you could only stand in the middle, but my bed was next to one of the front windows and I could see the ocean again. There was only one bedroom, and Larry and my father shared it. It had a double bed with a night stand on one side and a battered chest of drawers on the other side which they also shared. My father said it would be better if I didn't sleep in the same room as he did, and besides, Larry had already tested positive. I didn't mind. We seemed more like a family now, and I had taken to referring to Larry as "my uncle Larry" to people like Mrs. Evola and Bunny, but I didn't tell Larry. I wasn't sure he wanted to be my uncle.

23

BUNNY KNEW OCEAN PARK PIER like the back of his hand. He also knew the amusement park at Long Beach and the one at Venice. All of them were huge with roller coasters and bumper cars and a diving bell and whirl-a-gigs and popcorn and hot dog stands. They were best on weekends, Bunny said, but not much on weekdays. He spent every Saturday and Sunday at one or the other of them. Weekdays were for finding out stuff, he said. Where the back doors of the freak shows were and how to climb up into the web of timbers that supported the roller coaster without being seen.

We met that first Saturday at Ocean Park Pier in Santa Monica and took the Red Car to "The Pike," an amusement arcade at the Long Beach Pier. There was a freak show, a long low building with a painted sign that ran the length of it: STRANGE PEOPLE LIVING ODDITIES ALL ALIVE. Underneath the sign were paintings that looked about as stiff as the birds I had tried to draw in Arizona: Electra, dressed in a bathing suit, holding a glowing light bulb and a whirling electric fan; a sword swallower; the Headless Girl, a naked woman sitting sideways so you couldn't see her crotch and with no head—just a collar where her neck should have been with a stem rising out of it connected to two tubes, one hooked onto an oxygen tank, the other to a bottle filled with a fluid that looked like dog puke; a man with four legs; and a "snake man" who had writhing snakes for arms. Out front was an old guy on a pedestal with a microphone who continuously harangued the crowd, sailors in whites, lots of men and fewer girls, mostly with their arms linked through the arms of a sailor.

"Most of it's fake," Bunny said. "Except for the fat lady and the giant."

"How do you know?"

"I been inside. I snuck around back when there was nobody there. The headless girl is a naked girl who sits in a chair with her head in a clamp, and there's some mirrors and that other stuff that sits on a table. So when you look at her from the front, you don't see her head, just the tubes and stuff."

"You saw her naked?"

"No, but I saw her chair and the clamp and the table with that stuff and when I went around in front of the window you look through I could see the empty chair and the collar in the air above it."

"What about the snake man?"

"I don't know about him, but nobody's got snakes for arms. You can bet on that. Come on, let's go trolling."

I had no idea what he meant by that. We went to the end of the boardwalk next to the roller coaster and slid beneath the bottom rail, dropping the short distance to the sand. He disappeared under the boardwalk and I followed.

It wasn't completely dark underneath the boards, but dark enough so that I had a hard time making out Bunny. He was an indistinct shape crouched, waiting for me.

"Follow me," he said, and set off at a trot between the parallel rows of piers, the blackness on our left, the white sand on our right, broken by the steady wall of pilings.

"Keep your head down," he hissed.

Tarred beams were just above my head and long strings of dirt hung down through the spaces between the boards, brushing my face. Bunny ran in a Groucho Marx crouch, his feet sliding ahead in the soft sand, and when I said, "What are we doing," he hissed again without turning his head, "Shut up. You'll see."

Above us the roller coaster rumbled and shoes hit the boards, suddenly darkening the cracks between them. There was music from the carousel and the surf hissed, all combining to make a steady background noise that shut out everything, leaving us lurching down this half-dark corridor. The sand was soft and I kept slipping, going down on my hands and knees, lunging ahead, trying to keep up with Bunny.

He stopped and I ran into him, nearly knocking him over. In front of him was a body until I realized it was two bodies—a sailor on top of a girl, his sailor pants down around his knees, his pink behind barely visible in the half-dark.

Bunny yelled, "Ride him, cowboy!" and the sailor stopped moving, his head jerking around. We were silhouetted against the slatted light from the boards above us and the beach behind us, and for an instant I suppose he thought we were adults; but he got a better look and rolled off the woman, shouting, "You little bastards," struggling to pull his skivvies from around his knees. The woman scrambled to pull her dress down from where it was bunched across her stomach and the sailor, his pants now up around his waist, lunged out, trying to grab Bunny's ankle, but Bunny stepped back, banging into me.

"Wait'll I get my hands on you, you little bastard!" the sailor shouted again, rising; but the front flap of his sailor pants wasn't buttoned and they began to slide down again. He stood up to grab them, banging his head on the boardwalk and yelled, "Shit!"

The woman kept pleading, "Be quiet. Somebody will hear you," although with the roller coaster and the carousel and the noises from the beach and the surf, I didn't think he would have been heard unless somebody had their ear to the boardwalk.

"I don't care!" he yelled at her, slashing out again at Bunny, who took off down the dark sand again and I followed, my heart pounding. Behind us the sailor was still cursing and, out of the corner of my eye, I could see a man with a dog on a leash standing on the beach, bent forward, peering into the darkness under the boardwalk.

Bunny and I burst out into the sunlight at the end of the boardwalk and ran another fifty yards before we flopped on the hot sand.

"Jesus," Bunny said, "that was great."

"What were they doing?" knowing as I asked, what the answer was.

"Screwing. You gotta be kidding!"

"I knew that. I meant, what were they doing under the board-walk?" I was trying to cover my tracks.

"That's where they go. Sailors. They come off their ship for the day and if they get lucky they get a girl who will go down there with them." We leaned on our elbows, squinting out at the ocean. An excursion boat left the end of a narrow pier that jutted out into the water, crossing our line of sight, the rails lined with people. A dog worried a piece of seaweed in front of us, whipping the bulb end, growling as it thrashed its head from side to side.

"Sometimes," Bunny said to the ocean, "I'll run the whole length of the boardwalk a couple of times a day for a whole weekend and not catch anybody. Today we got lucky. It's like fishing. That's why I call it trolling."

"Why?"

"I just told you, dummy!"

"No, I mean why catch them?"

"It's fun to watch old people get pissed off."

"That guy wasn't so old."

"Yeah, but he was old enough. Come on. Let's sneak under the roller coaster."

The roller coaster was built out on a pier that branched off from the main boardwalk. From the top you could see up and down the coast and all the way inland to the San Gabriel Mountains. But Bunny wasn't interested in riding the coaster. He was interested in what lay underneath.

The space under the roller coaster was closed off with a high wooden fence, but Bunny knew where the loose boards were and we slipped inside. Above us the roller coaster rattled, climbing into the first long ascent, the wheels steadily clacking; then with a roar it plummeted in a diving crescendo of shrieks, squealing wheels, and creaking timbers. It sounded as if it were about to come apart.

"We got to be quick," Bunny shouted over the noise. "If the guys who run it see us in here, run like hell!" He crouched over and began to duckwalk across the planked surface, his head bent forward intently.

"What are you looking for?" I asked.

"Money. Change. All kinds of stuff falls out of people's pockets. That's why they don't want us here." He looked up across the boards in front of him. As he suddenly scooted on all fours, I saw the wallet lying open in the shadow of the fence.

"Jackpot!" He stuffed the wallet in his pocket.

"Come on!" He turned and headed for the fence in a crouching run.

Behind Duke's Corn-on-the-Cob we examined the wallet. It had forty-two dollars in it, four tens, and two ones, a photograph of a sailor and a girl that had been taken in a booth, and a military ID card that showed it belonged to Machinist Mate First Class Duane Davis.

Bunny handed me two tens and a one. "We share," he said. "We'll dump the wallet in a mailbox. He'll get it back."

"It's a lot of money," said, fingering the bills., "Shouldn't we try to get the money to him, too?"

"Jeez, are you out of your mind? If we leave the money in the wallet some mailman is gonna take it. This is our lucky day. Let's get something to eat," He stuffed the bills in one pocket, the wallet in another. "What a day! We caught a sailor under the boardwalk and we found some treasure. Hey! Maybe this wallet belongs to that creep we caught with his pants down. Wouldn't that be great?" He grinned from ear to ear.

Bunny Smith had huge ears that stuck out on either side of his head like fleshy flaps, spiky red hair, and an expression on his face that made him seem perpetually startled. I would discover that he could use that look to good advantage when he was caught by an adult. It was as if he could not have done what they had caught him red-handed doing. He seemed so surprised that they relaxed their grip, thinking perhaps what they had, in fact, seen, was not the case at all—that they had the wrong kid, so complete seemed his bewilderment. In that instant of relaxation, Bunny would bolt.

We ate hot dogs and salt-water taffy and drank sodas and rode the bumper cars, deliberately aiming at each other from opposite sides of the rink, trying for violent head-on crashes until the attendant threw us out. We rode the roller coaster and Bunny squirmed out from under the safety bar to stand up at the very moment the coaster crested the top. He raised his arms and shouted, "Good-bye cruel world!" and a man in the seat behind us grabbed him by the shoulders and slammed him down into the seat, yelling, "You crazy kid! You trying to get yourself killed?"

Bunny yelled something back but by then we were rushing down the steepest part and the noise of the wheels and the screams of the crowed drowned it out. I vowed that the next time I, too, would stand up, but we were grabbed by the ticket taker as we tried for another ride and roughly shaken.

"You little brats know better than that!" he yelled. "Don't come around here again, do you hear?"

In the shooting arcade Bunny missed his first shot, then shot out five targets in a row and won an ugly orange bear which he said he would give to his sister.

"How did you learn to shoot so well?" I asked.

"Back home in Oklahoma I had a .22, " he said. "I used to shoot rabbits and squirrels. But these guns are fixed. They got the sights turned one way or the other. You got to take one shot and see where it hits. Then you aim the opposite of whichever side it hits."

I was sorry when the sky turned dark and people began to straggle up off the beach, clutching sandy blankets, their faces red. The lights went on up and down the boardwalk and the music of the carousel seemed louder. Now sailors strolled with an arm around a girl's waist and the water turned nearly black. The surf disappeared and only the slap of water told us the ocean was beyond the strip of now-deserted beach.

I didn't want the day to end. All of the pent-up energy that had been tamped down during those three months at Metzenbaum's was bubbling up, and I felt as if I would never need to sleep again. But Bunny had to go home.

"My did will whip me good if I miss supper," he said.

"Does he know you're here?"

"He says it don't make any difference what I do so long as I don't get hurt or hurt anybody else or lie or steal and I'm home by supper."

"We stole that wallet."

"No, we didn't!" Bunny protested. "We found it! Finders keepers. That's the law."

I got on the Red Car heading north to Santa Monica, leaving him to wait for the trolley that would take him to Willowbrook. We promised to meet again at Ocean Park on Saturday.

24

THE FOLLOWING SATURDAY, BUNNY showed me how to ding the trolleys. We waited until a car came to a stop, then slipped behind the car and he grabbed the heavy rope attached to the trolley pole that reached from the top of the car to the overhead electric wire. There was a groove that the wire sat in, and when he gave the rope a hard enough jerk, the pole came down. Pulling it to one side, he let go and the springs on the pole shot it back up. It grazed the electric wire in a shower of sparks, then bobbed into the air above the wire. The motorman, finding the car dead, came out the door and around to the back to re-set the pole and we scooted around the opposite side of the car, crouched down, and slipped inside.

I started for the far back, but Bunny motioned for us to sit next to the rear exit. "Just in case somebody tells on us, we can get out quick," he said.

When we got to Glendale, where the Yellow Line intersected, Bunny showed me how to ride the cowcatchers. The Yellow Line had older cars with catchers that looked like bed springs slanted out in front and back of the double-ended cars, and it was easy enough to run and throw yourself at the one on the rear end just as the car pulled away. Of course, it was dangerous, and several times cars came up behind and honked at the motorman, pointing at the back of the car. When that happened, we jumped off at the next stop and waited around for another car.

Shortly before noon a police car pulled up behind us. When the trolley stopped, Bunny leaped off and sprinted for the corner, but the cop was already out of his car and had Bunny by the arm before he had gone ten steps. I was scared and stood there, paralyzed, as the cop shook Bunny by the shoulders.

"What the hell's wrong with you kids?" he said. "You want to kill yourselves?"

Bunny's face took on that wide-eyed look and suddenly he was loose and running.

"Dammit!" the cop yelled. He reached out and grabbed me. Unlike Bunny, I hadn't been planning my escape.

"What's your name?" he demanded,

"Metzenbaum," I stammered.

"Who's your pal?"

"I don't know. He was just a guy I was riding the trolleys with."

"You expect me to believe that?" He tightened his grip on my arm. "Well, Metzenbaum, we're going to find out where you live and we're going to find your folks, and you aren't going to ride the back end of no more trolleys." He started toward the police car with me in tow. I could imagine being taken to jail and waiting while my father was summoned.

I think at that moment I crossed over into the adult world. I suddenly wasn't a scared kid at the mercy of events over which I had no control. I realized I could shape events to my advantage, if only I used my wits. Up to that point I had invented stories and small lies, but only out a sense of urgency or boredom. In my child's world, they had been a way to escape punishment, or kill time; but I knew the adult world lied regularly, not just to get out of a tough scrape, but as an expedient. My literary heroes had not just written stories. They had written elaborate lies, constructing worlds in which one could live another life. You didn't have to play with the cards that were dealt to you. You could invent your own hand and play it instead.

"Please sir," I said. I tried to fill my voice with the tremolo of fear, although I'm sure part of it was real. "I live in Long Beach. My father's overseas in the Navy and my mother works. I promise never to ride the trolleys again if you'll let me go home. I promise."

I knew it was at least a forty-five minute drive to Long Beach, and I was sure the police department of Glendale had neither the time to drive me there nor the inclination to keep a twelve-year-old while a mother was summoned from work. Of course I didn't live in Long Beach. But the Navy part would appeal to his sense of patriotism. He looked carefully at me.

"You could get yourself killed, you know. Or get a leg cut off. It happens."

I knew then he was going to let me go.

We waited in the car until the next trolley came along and he watched while I boarded it. I could hardly wait to tell Bunny how I had talked my way out of my jam.

I decided that Bunny would head for his house, so I left the trolley at San Pedro. It occurred to me that I could avoid the fare if I used my new-found ability and hitched a ride on the Red Car that was bound for Willowbrook.

The Red Cars were harder because the catcher was halfway under the car and it took me quite awhile before I got up the courage to try one of those. Just as it pulled out of the San Pedro stop, I slipped onto the rear catcher, hanging on sideways with one leg hooked up over the top of the grill. As the car picked up speed, the tracks slid by under my rear end with nothing to catch me if I dropped off.

What I didn't realize was that this Red Car had no trolley poles. I had hitched a ride on an express car that switched to the Southern Pacific electric rail. It would hit sixty miles an hour before it came to the first stop at Dominguez Junction. I hung on in the roaring slip-stream, scared out of my wits while we rocked back and forth, my eyes shut against the dirt that whirled around me. I got off ten minutes later, certain that I'd escaped death by inches. I suppose I presented quite a sight to anyone who might have seen me: a small body pressed like an insect against the grill, like an afterthought, on the trolley that slammed down the line, the motorman and passengers oblivious to the terror I felt, my hands clamped to the rusty steel until I had no feeling in them. I had, quite by accident, tested my limits and found I could go a step further than I had previously thought possible

25

AT THE FAR NORTHERN end of Santa Monica was a row of mansions with curving driveways that came in under porticoed entrances. Some were white stucco, brilliant in the sun, with red tiled roofs, and others were brick with porches that ran all the way around them, deep and cool in their shade. Some had lawns with sprinklers that were turned on in the early morning and in the evening after the sun had gone off them, and on hot evenings it was good to stand next to them. They reminded me of the lawns in Illinois and the grass in the park along Lake Michigan, and I remembered a picnic our family had taken on a beach there, with the city at our backs, the blue lake stretched out in front of us.

There was a walkway that ran along the bluff behind the Santa Monica houses and I sometimes took it in my efforts to avoid policemen and truant officers, who I imagined were around every corner. Once I was on the walk behind these grand houses, I was hidden from the street and rarely met anyone other than old ladies.

One afternoon as I passed one of the houses, I heard a piano. The notes came from somewhere far inside a house, drifting out toward the ocean, repeating sometimes as if the pianist wanted to get it just right and then continuing slowly, drifting with the tide of the afternoon. I knew it was a classical piece. I had never paid much attention to classical music, but there was something about this song that stopped me on the sidewalk, caught between the row of handsome houses and the ocean with its cries of solitary bathers below the bluff faint and faraway. The melody was faintly familiar. I stood, listening, trying to remember;

and then I felt it was, in some way, like one of Larry's records. Vaguely like a song he and my father had danced to in Metzenbaum's cottage. The records and the record player were in the apartment. Sometimes Larry got them out in the evening and we listened to them although he and my father didn't dance. I wanted to go back to the apartment and find the melody that was floating across the back yards of the rich.

I knew my father would be home, resting on the sofa near the window. I would tell him school had been let out an hour early so the teachers would have conferences with parents. Larry would still be at work.

Neither of them heard me open the door to the apartment and step inside.

They were in the doorway to their little bedroom, pressed against the jamb, or at least my father was. Larry's body obscured my father and all I could see was one of my father's hands flat against the wall on one side, the other reaching up to hold the edge of the half-closed door. His fingers were white, as if he were gripping it for dear life, afraid to let go in case he should fall a long way. My first thought was that Larry was holding him up and that he was unconscious, but Larry turned his head to bury his face in the hollow of my father's neck and in that instant I saw his face, his eyes closed, his mouth open. My father's hand came away from the door, cupping the back of Larry's head, and I could see that his eyes, too, were closed.

I wanted to leave but I was afraid I would make a noise and he would open his eyes and see me standing there. I had entered a scene where I did not belong, had entered on the wrong cue and could not leave the stage, yet had nothing to say or do.

I carefully backed out of the door and closed it so that it made no sound. I tip-toed back down the stairs, then slammed the front door, knowing it would raise a shout from Mrs. Evola, and clumped my way up the stairs as loudly as I could.

"Hey! I'm home!" I shouted. Below me, Mrs. Evola's door opened and she stuck her head out into the stairwell.

"You! Tommy!" she yelled. "What's the matter with you? You make more noise than a drunk sailor!"

"Sorry, Mrs. Evola," I called down. I opened the door to our apartment.

My father was on the couch and Larry was putting on his sweater.

"What are you doing home so early?" my father asked.

"They let us out an hour early so they could have parent conferences."

"When do I get mine?"

"Oh, this is just for kids who have problems and the teachers want to talk to their mothers. You don't need to go. I'm doing great."

"So how come we never see you doing homework?" Larry asked.

"Because I get it done at the library. Can I listen to your records?"

"Sure," he said.

"The teacher played some music for us at school today. It was one of those orchestra pieces, but it sounded like one of your records." I tried to hum the melody that was still running through my head.

"That's 'Clair de Lune,'" he said.

"No, I don't mean the name of the singer. I mean the name of the song. Do you know it?"

Larry laughed. "'Clair de Lune' is the name of the song," he said. "It means 'in the moonlight.'"

"How come you're not at work?"

"I came home to have lunch with your dad. I'm working the late shift."

"Long lunch." I said, and immediately regretted it.

"What's that supposed to mean?" Larry stood, smoothing his sweater with his hands.

"Nothing." I had overstepped. I was caught between the blurry face of my mother in the park on the edge of Lake Michigan and this man who had taken her place. My father spoke.

"Get out the records and we'll see if we can find your tune," he said. "Don't worry about us, Larry. We'll boil some hot dogs and eat like pigs."

"Maybe you'll find some homework you forgot to do," Larry said, still looking at me.

"Maybe." I wasn't ready to surrender yet. The problem was, I didn't know who the enemy was. I wanted to say, *I saw what you were doing!* I wanted to clear the air, to find out where I stood in all of this, to tell them I wasn't going to school, to have someone tell me how sick my father really was, whether or not he was dying, why my mother had so readily left me with this frail man who seemed unable to leave the sofa except to grapple with Larry in a doorway. I had read that sometimes tuberculosis patients felt great surges of passion in the midst of heightened fevers, and I wondered if this was what had happened.

But nothing came. "That sweater looks great," I said to Larry.

He smiled. "Eddie, we better watch out. This one has got a smooth tongue."

I didn't get out the record player. My father didn't seem to notice. I went downstairs and knocked on Mrs. Evola's door and when she came to the door I apologized for my noise.

"That's okay," she said. "You're a good boy for saying so. Come in and have some popcorn."

Mrs. Evola lived on the ground floor with a front parlor filled with little tables that had button gardens arranged on them and a parrot in the front window. Newspapers were spread over the floor under his cage and the whole place smelled of bird and popcorn and garlic. Her kitchen was lined with shelves filled with vegetables she canned herself, and I never saw her dressed in anything other than black shoes, black stockings, a black dress and a flowered smock over the whole outfit. Short, dumpy, she stumped around the yard, in and out of her back door, the pockets of the smock bulging with tools: pliers and screwdrivers to fix a broken light switch, or pruning shears to cut back the masses of geraniums that were banked against the house. She made popcorn by dumping olive oil into a dented pot, waiting until it began to smoke, and then throwing in a handful of kernels and holding the lid over it while we waited for the popping to begin.

Then we sat in the parlor while she worked on her latest button garden. Each one began with a block of wood. She glued buttons to the block, sorting through several flat tins crammed with thousands of cast-off buttons.

"This one is the castle garden," she said. She had stacked white shirt buttons into columns through which wound a pathway of square black-and-white buttons, like paving stones. "This," she said, holding up a large iridescent mother-of-pearl button, "is going to be the fish pond but I need grass around the edge. Help me find some green buttons, Tommy."

I searched through one tin while she rummaged in the other. Gradually a pile of variegated green grew between us.

"Did you know my father is sick?" I asked.

"Yes."

"Do you know what he has?"

"Yes."

I sifted through the buttons. "How about this one?"

"Too big."

"How come you let us stay here if you know what he has?"

"When I was a girl in Italy, lots of women in my village had consumption. Mostly it was girls who got it. I didn't. I don't think I'm gonna get it now. Not at my age."

"Do most people die from it"

"Lots don't. You afraid your poppa is gonna die?"

"I don't know."

"He says he's gonna go to some fancy place out in Azusa where they'll cure him."

"The City of Hope. It's in Arcadia."

"*Citta di Speranza*. Nice name."

"Do you have any kids?"

"They're all grown up. I got two boys who work in the shipyards in San Pedro. They're both married. Sundays I go to one house or the other. Summertime they're all down here for the beach, Kids all over the place. You folks will be gone by then."

Bruno the parrot began a low growling sound, then burst into a hacking cough. He sounded exactly like the men in my father's cottage at Metzenbaum's, a hacking man's cough that reverberated throughout the room.

"Bruno!" Mrs. Evola said sharply. "Stop that or I'll put you to bed!" Bruno cocked his head and made a regular parrot squawk.

"He got that from my husband, God rest him. He coughed a lot at the end. Bruno drove me nuts. He learned to cough and sometimes I'd come into the room, thinking poor Ernie was coughing his lungs out, only it was that ugly parrot."

"Did your husband die of tuberculosis?"

"No. He just wore out. Parrots don't wear out so easy. They last a long time. Don't you, Bruno?" she said, raising her voice.

The parrot cocked his head again, but said nothing.

"Do men ever marry other men, Mrs. Evola?"

"Blessed Mary, what kind of a question is that?"

"I just wondered."

"Well, you don't need to wonder about that one. Men marry women and that's that. It's God's law, so just don't ask that foolish question again or people are liable to think there's something wrong with you."

"What if a man liked another man a whole lot. I mean really liked him."

Mrs. Evola stopped rummaging through the tin of buttons she held in her hand. "Then they should be the best of friends, like brothers, and that's that."

"Can brothers hold hands and stuff like that?"

She held up a tiny green button and touched the back of it with a bit of glue on a pointed stick. "In the old country, boys could hold hands and nobody thought anything about it. Sometimes I would see them in the square in the evening, whole bunches of them, holding hands, their arms around each others' shoulders." Her voice began to fade as if she were going someplace and her voice was following her. She stuck the button to the edge of the pond on the wooden block. "But not here," she said, her voice back with a sharpness. "Not here. Ever."

26

ON SUNDAY I GOT permission to have dinner with Bunny's family. Mrs. Smith invited my father and Larry, too, but I told her they couldn't come because my uncle worked as a cook on Sundays in a restaurant in Santa Monica and my father wasn't feeling well. I sat on the back steps with Mr. Smith and we watched Bunny who was trying to teach the cat to sit up and beg.

"You got about as much chance of teaching him to do that as you have to make a pig fly," Mr. smith called out.

Bunny pulled the cat up on its haunches, held out his forefinger with a blob of lard on it until the cat began to lick it, but the cat collapsed in a soft heap as soon as the lard was gone.

"Can I ask you something?" I said.

"Fire away." He tapped his pack of Lucky Strikes against the step, then snapped it so that one of the cigarettes shot up from the open pack.

"Is it okay for men to dance with each other?"

He slowly withdrew the cigarette and examined it.

"You mean two men like me?"

"Yes." I could tell that he was examining the question the same way he was examining the cigarette. He knew what it was. That wasn't the problem.

"You seen two men dancing together someplace?"

"No," I lied. "I just wondered. I mean, if I wanted to learn to dance, wouldn't it be okay if another guy showed me how?"

He touched the cigarette to his lips, snapped a wooden kitchen match with one calloused thumb and said, "Be better if you had your mother or a sister show you how. That's more the way it ought to be done." Then, as if he suddenly remembered that I had told him my mother was dead, he added, "You could borrow Mrs. Smith or Enid. You don't mind if Tommy borrows your sister to learn how to dance, do you?" he called out to Bunny, chuckling as he did so.

"Enid can't dance," Bunny said.

"Well, I'm sure your mother would oblige." He took a drag on the cigarette, letting the smoke come out of his mouth and nose at the same time. He looked remarkably like a weather-beaten dragon at that moment.

"But what if I didn't have someone like her to teach me?" I persisted. "Wouldn't it be okay if I got my father or my uncle to teach me?"

"I suppose so," Mr. Smith said.

"How about if I were your age and I wanted to learn to dance and didn't have a wife to teach me?"

I continued to look out into the yard at Bunny and the cat, but I could tell by the sound of his voice that he had turned to face me.

"You're certainly full of questions this afternoon. You trust me on this one, young man: You want to learn to dance, you're better off borrowing Mrs. S. She's a pretty good dancer."

"My uncle is a good dancer," I said. "He taught my father to dance."

"Is that so?" The cat was trying to get away now and Bunny had it by the scruff of the neck.

"He's got lots of girlfriends," I added. Something in Mr. Smith's voice prompted the invention and I could suddenly see legions of women waiting in line to dance with Larry but they all looked like the Andrews sisters. "He goes dancing with them just about every weekend."

"I'm glad to hear that," Mr. Smith said. He focused on Bunny. "You let that cat go," he said, "or I'll grab you by the skin of your neck and we'll see how quick you learn to beg."

Bunny let loose of the cat and it darted under the porch.

Mrs. Smith was calling us from the kitchen and Mr. Smith rose to go inside. "This uncle of yours. Is he related to that aunt who maybe lives in Compton?"

"No, he lives with us. He's my mother's brother. He's a cook in a restaurant."

"I believe you told us that," he said. "You want to learn to dance, you ask Mrs. Smith. The boy's part isn't the same as the girl's part. You'll find it easier." That, apparently, was the end of the conversation. But now I knew that the connection between my father and Larry wasn't something I could easily talk about to anyone else. And I had been right when I referred to him as my uncle. Somehow it made it less awkward. I resolved to ask Mrs. Smith to teach me to dance. I had no desire to learn, but it seemed the prudent thing to do.

27

I SPENT THE DAY at the Griffith Park Zoo, staying until closing time, which meant that I didn't get home until it had turned dark. I expected my father to chew me out, and I rehearsed a library excuse; but he only said, "When Larry gets here, I've got some news." He seemed suffused with excitement and I knew enough about his disease to know it went in cycles and his energy might simply be one of those highs that would be followed by rising fever and a sudden descent into torpor. Impending news might mean anything. Perhaps he had been called by the City of Hope. Worse, we would move again.

But when Larry got home, my father announced he had a job.

"Good Christ, Eddie! How? Where?"

"I called Santa Anita racetrack and told them I was looking for work and they told me to come out and I rode the Pacific Electric right there. It's in Arcadia, almost to Duarte." Did you know you could ride those trolley cars all the way across Los Angeles? It took an hour, and I was there, and they hired me as a clubhouse runner."

"What's a clubhouse runner?" I asked.

"I told them I was a teller at Washington Park and Arlington Park, but they didn't need tellers. They made a telephone call to Washington Park and Will Johnson, my old supervisor there, told them I was okay; so they gave me the runner's job. It was all they had open."

"Yes," I persisted, "but you can't run."

"There's no running, Tommy. I take bets in the clubhouse and take them down to the tellers. I make the bets for them and come back up. Nine trips a day. That's it!"

"Why don't they make their own bets?"

"Because they're rich and they want to sit at a table and drink fancy drinks and they don't want to stand in line with the two-dollar bettors. Do you know who I saw today?"

"I'm afraid to ask," Larry said.

"George Jessel. He owns horses. And Don Ameche. He owns horses, too. Both of them were sitting them big as life."

I had not seen my father so animated since we left Metzenbaum's.

"Eddie," Larry said, "You can't work. You're sick."

"The Santa Anita meet only goes another two months. It's easy work. I can do it. I'll be able to save what I make, Between the two of us we can have enough for me to spend six months at the City of Hope. Besides, I can't just sit here all day. I feel good right now. I can do it, I know. I'm not coughing. There's no blood."

His forehead was shining with sweat from the kitchen light. It looked as if it had been oiled, and his features were sharp, drawn tightly over the bones of his face.

28

THERE WAS A KNOCK on the door of our apartment and when I went to answer it, Mrs. Evola was there. "There's a man downstairs who says he knows you people," she said.

"What is it?" my father asked.

"A man downstairs," she repeated, raising her voice so he could hear. "He says he knows you, but I wasn't sure I should let him in."

"What's his name?" my father asked.

"He didn't say. But he looks awful rough, so I told him to wait on the steps." She stood back, her message complete.

"We'll take a look," my father said, and stepped past her. I followed.

In the darkness on the steps was Willie. He had on the same clothes I had last seen him in, but his cowboy boots had the soles taped to them with layers of adhesive tape that wrapped around each foot, and his plaid coat was stained and matted. His hair was longer than it had been, lank, down around his face and over his shoulders.

"Good God, Willie," my father said. "Where's your friend?"

"I left him in L.A." he said. "I don't like to ask this, but we need some money to go back to Vallecitos."

"Is the Chief all right?" I asked.

"He's okay. He's in a shelter downtown. They got one that takes Indians."

"Come on up," my father said. "You need a hot cup of coffee." He held the door open and Willie went past us. He smelled bad, not just sweat, but something else, like spoiled meat and sour milk.

In the light of the apartment he looked even worse. His skin was splotchy and his face was puffed out. There was a bruise on the side of his face, a purple discoloring that gave him a lopsided look. He sat gingerly in a chair, as if afraid he would dirty it, and blew across the hot coffee that Larry gave him.

"How did you find us?" my father asked.

"Lucky, I guess. I came out to where we got left off and I started asking around. I spent two, maybe three days asking, but nobody knew you in Santa Monica, and I just about gave up; but I hung around the Pier and I panhandled some and some fellows knew Tommy. Then it seemed like a bunch of people there knew Tommy and I found a kid who knew where you lived."

My father looked curiously at me.

"I'm sorry to come here like this. We're at the end of our rope. If you've got ten dollars you can lend us, it'll get us started. We'll pay you back. I'll send the money."

Los Angeles had been a bust for Willie and the Chief, too.

"What about the movies?" I asked.

"Bullshit, kid stuff. It's all lies. There aren't any Indians in those movies. Just fat white guys in brown paint."

"No jobs, either, I suppose," my father said.

"Not that we could find. The oil jobs go to the crackers from the South who got experience on the rigs and me and the Chief don't exactly look too good any more." He grinned for the first time. "Los Angeles ain't a good place to drink in. Too many sharp edges when you fall down."

Larry made him some scrambled eggs and he drank more coffee and my father gave him a twenty-dollar bill and wished him luck. And he was gone.

Then my father turned to me.

"Got a lot of friends at the Pier, have you?"

"I spend every Saturday there."

"How's school going?"

"Fine."

"I grew up in a little coal mining town downstate from Chicago. You knew that, didn't you?"

I nodded. I wondered what he was getting at.

"They had these slag tips around the mines. We weren't supposed to play on them. They were like little mountains. Like ice cream cones upside down. The reason the company didn't want us there was because sometimes they shifted and you could get crushed when big chunks of slag came loose. You understand?"

I nodded, but I had no idea what he was getting at. Larry was wiping a plate with a dish towel, watching us.

"Some of the kids used to go there anyway. There were pools of black water that came up to the edges of the slag tips and bigger boys swam in them. I don't know how they did it. The water must have had all kinds of stuff in it. It wasn't scummy or anything like that—it was just black and awful looking. But whatever it was didn't stick to you. The water ran off just like regular water. I wouldn't go near it.

"They had an old watchman on the weekends to keep the kids away. But during the week he knew the kids were in school so he didn't leave his little shed. The best time to go to the slag tips was during school."

Now I knew where he was going. Larry had turned and was putting the plate and cup away. He folded the towel neatly and hung it in front of the stove. I watched him. I knew my father was looking directly at me.

"I went there once when I was about your age. We caught water dogs and roasted potatoes in a fire we made out of timbers and some of the boys had gunny sacks. They picked among the slag for lumps of coal that had been missed. They would sell them for extra money. But mostly I watched the boys swim until the watchman must have seen the smoke from the fire because he showed up. They all grabbed their clothes and ran up into the slag tip and they rolled chunks of slag down at the old man, and he cursed them and he yelled that he'd get the police. I got scared and hid in a crevice. I stayed there until it got dark, and then I worked my way down and went home. My father was waiting for me. He used his belt on me. I kept telling him that I hadn't done anything wrong, but he just kept yelling that he might work in a hole in the ground, but he wasn't dumb. That was the last time I played hooky."

"I don't think you're dumb," I said.

"I don't think you are, either." He took off his glasses and cleaned them with the napkin that lay on the table. He polished them meticulously. His fingers were slender and his nails neatly clipped. I wondered what my grandfather's hands had looked like. I had never thought of my grandfather, who died before I was born, as a coal miner. I had never really thought of him as anything.

Larry came and stood behind my father. He leaned his head forward until his chin rested on my father's shoulder, looking directly at me. "Jesus Christ," he said. "You two. If you aren't the damnedest pair."

29

I AWOKE TO RAIN. It pattered against the window, and in my half-sleep it was like Dr. Metzenbaum's fingers tapping the glass. Outside, the ocean was flat and gray and the sky was the same color as the water. Everything was sodden. It had been threatening rain for several days, but now it was here, a steady emptying of the dense clouds that obscured the horizon. It meant that the Pier would not open, the corn-on-the-cob and the hot dog stands would remain shuttered for the day, and if it continued on into the weekend, the roller coaster would be idle.

I dressed and ate breakfast as usual, and asked my father if the horses ran in the rain.

"Sure," he said. "Some horses run better in the rain. Not so many people, though. It'll be a quiet day. You off to school?"

"Yes."

"For sure?"

"Yes," I said. "Where else would I go?"

But I didn't go to school. I went to the Pier and walked for a while among the soggy papers and watched the rain beat on the ocean. I found a hot dog stand still open and bought a hot dog and ate it under the opened widow flap. Then I got on a Red Car and rode south and transferred east. Gullies that had been dry ever since I had arrived were suddenly full, muddy brown, trash floating in the eddies. The windows of the car were streaked with rain and a windshield wiper swept back and forth in front of the driver. The bottoms of the windows steamed and I thought of trying to find Bunny, but I knew that on a day like this he would be in school. I wondered if Willie and the Chief had gone back to Vallecitos or if they had drunk up the twenty dollars my father had given them.

My throat began to hurt and by the time I had taken a car back to the coast, I was hot, and could barely swallow. I went back to the apartment and took off my clothes, crawling into my bed where I lay sweating, waiting for someone to come home.

My father was the first to arrive in late afternoon, and when he saw me in my bed, he knew I was sick.

He made me open my mouth, looked in my throat, and made some tea with lemon and so much sugar that it was almost like syrup. "Drink this," he said. "It'll make you feel better."

"It's only a sore throat," he told Larry later. Larry made tomato soup from a can and I sipped at it, but it was raw in my throat and I ate the saltine crackers and nothing else. I felt better and lay there, listening to them talk.

"I did something today that Earl Joyner used to do at Washington Park," my father said.

"Who's Earl Joyner?"

"A guy I knew back east. He was the clubhouse runner when I was a teller at Washington Park."

"What was that?"

"I covered a bet."

"What's that mean, Eddie?"

"It means that a guy made a bet I thought was really stupid, a long shot that had no business running in the mud, and it was a sure loser, so I didn't place his bet. I kept his money."

"Jesus, Eddie." Larry's voice was suddenly alert, full of concern. "What would have happened if he had won?"

"Then I would have been long gone from the race track and he would have wondered where his thousand bucks was."

"Whatever possessed you to do that?"

"He made a ten-dollar bet on a hundred-to-one shot, and I thought to myself, it's chicken feed to him, but it's damn near a day at the City of Hope; and Earl did it all the time, so why not." He was smoothing his hair back on both sides of his head with his hands. His voice had a hard edge to it, an anger that filled his soft voice.

"I'm know I'm not getting better. I know I need treatment. I heard from some people that they've got some new wonder drug they're using there. It's supposed to cure TB. I don't know whether to believe them or not. They're all quacks. I think they just take your money and let you lie around and wait to see if you die or get well. But I can't just keep going this way. There are times when I can hardly make it back up to the clubhouse, And I'm coughing again."

I turned on my side toward the window. It was dark now, but I could hear the steady rush of the ocean beyond the streaky pane. I did not want to hear any more. Perhaps I would go to school tomorrow, tell them we had moved back from Arizona, get a job after school. I had ten dollars in change from the money that Bunny and I had found under the roller coaster. I would give that to my father.

"Earl said he doubled his salary that way. He'd cover dumb long shots and a few small bets that he had the cash to pay off. He said he could make twice what he usually made in a day."

"Don't they ask for their ticket when you come back?"

"I was slow with it. And nobody wants a ticket for a horse that's lost. If they did, I'd give them an old one. They just tear them up anyway."

"What if they look at it?" Larry wasn't convinced.

"Look, there's a risk. I know that."

"Won't the track find out?"

"Not unless somebody blows the whistle on me. Or they send up a stooge to check me out. They do that sometimes to make sure the runners aren't making book. But they called Washington Park and I got a good recommendation, so I ought to be okay."

"You shouldn't be working at all," Larry said.

"What do you want me to do? Lie here and look at the ocean all day? For Chrissake, what's the point in that? Are you expecting to inherit money or something? How the hell are we going to get enough money ahead if I don't work?"

"You could go to the county hospital. They've got a TB ward there."

"And lie around in a roomful of lungers waiting to die? I'd have a better chance if I went to the park and bet hundred-to-one shots all day. Larry, don't you see? I can't just wait."

"I've got ten dollars," I said. "You can have that."

My father looked at me, startled, as if I had suddenly appeared in the room.

"I can get a job, too. I can get a paper route."

"Good God, Tommy," he said. "You don't have to do that." His voice lost its hard edge. "Besides, things are going to be okay. You wait and see."

Of course, I didn't believe that. Like the cop in Glendale, I wanted to believe promises of good things to come, but I knew better.

I remembered Tiny telling me that the Walapai shamans blew on sick people to the accompaniment of rattling gourds, then sucked out the disease-causing object.

"Those old guys are scary," Tiny had said. "They get to puffing out their breath and rattling those gourds and their eyes look all spooky, and then they suck some part of the body, like maybe the stomach, and you'd think they'd suck the guts right through the skin. Leave a big black mark that won't go away for days."

"Did it work?" I had asked.

"Don't ask me. Sometimes something works if you want it to bad enough."

I wanted desperately for my father to be well. Larry had said that Willie was a Walapai. Maybe he knew how to suck TB from a man's body.

30

ON SATURDAY AFTERNOON a truck full of school desks came down to the beach. They set them up in neat rows on the sand, just like a classroom, with a teacher's desk in front, a blackboard hung from two poles driven into the sand, and a globe on a stand. An American flag on a pole behind the teacher's desk completed the scene.

A man in slacks and a white shirt with his tie pulled loose began grabbing kids in their bathing suits. "Come on," he said, when he saw Bunny and me. "We're going to take a picture that will be in newspapers all over the country. Here's your chance to be famous."

It only took him ten minutes to round up thirty-five kids who all stood next to their desks while a young woman in a one-piece bathing suit stood in front of us as if she were the teacher.

A crowd gathered and a man called out, ""I never had a teacher who looked that good. If I had, I'd still be in school!" and the crowd laughed. Somebody else called out, "What's this all about?"

"Chamber of Commerce," the photographer said, squinting through the camera on a tripod behind the teacher. We all pretended to say the Pledge of Allegiance, putting our hands over our hearts, and then he took some pictures of us with our hands raised while the bathing beauty teacher pointed to the globe. Then it was over.

"That's it, kids," the photographer said, packing away the camera while the truck driver began loading up the desks again.

We crowded around the photographer. His shirt had large dark circles of sweat under each armpit. "When will this be in the papers?" We pestered him with questions. "What paper will it be in?"

"The funny papers," he said. "How the hell do I know? I just take 'em."

The photograph appeared in the *Los Angeles Times* the following week with a story about the unusually warm weather and an interview with a man from Long Beach who had moved from Iowa where he had been a snowplow driver. The story didn't actually say we were holding class on the beach. The caption read, "Santa Monica school children gather in an impromptu classroom on the beach." But Larry and my father immediately assumed that it was my class and those were my classmates and the young woman in front was my teacher.

Larry was the first to see the picture, bringing home the paper from his job at the diner.

"Hey, look who's famous," he shouted as he came into the apartment that night, dropping the paper on the table in front of my father. "How come you never said anything, Sport?"

I looked over my father's shoulder to see the picture, me in the second row, my hand raised, and Bunny next to me, his ears sticking out like a galleon under full sail. My father read the article carefully, then turned to me.

"Quite a nice-looking teacher you've got. If I had to look at her I guess I'd be in class every single day. Of course, teachers never dressed that way when I was in school."

"She doesn't dress that way every day," I said. Suddenly she was my teacher and these were my classmates. "Besides, we don't go down to the beach to have class. That was just a publicity stunt for the Chamber of Commerce."

"What's her name?"

"Who?"

"Your teacher, of course."

"Miss Osbourne." The name of Robert Louis Stevenson's wife, the one who nursed him back from his hemorrhage came out of my mouth. "She's from Indiana." That much was true, Fanny Osbourne had been born in Indiana.

"I thought your teacher was an older woman."

"That was Mrs. Gudgeon. We called her Mrs. Curmudgeon. She was in a car accident in Bakersfield and Miss Osbourne took her place."

"How come you never mentioned that?"

"I don't know. I guess I never thought you'd be interested."

My father looked again at the picture. "Who's the kid with the big ears?"

"Bunny Smith. He's from Oklahoma., He's my best friend at school."

"How come you don't bring him around here?"

"Because you're sick."

"What do you mean?"

"People won't want to be around me if they find out you've got TB. I guess they think they'll catch it."

"Jesus Christ, do you tell them I've got TB?"

"No. I tell them you work at the race track."

Larry came to my rescue. "Seems like everybody in California is from someplace else. If the people at Metzenbaum's see that picture of you on the beach in your bathing suit in December, they'll probably all be on the next train tomorrow. And now, in honor of the fact that Tommy is the first world-famous person in this family, look what I liberated from work."

He set a package of newspaper on the table and unwrapped it. Inside was half a cherry pie, still in its tin plate. "Actually, I didn't liberate it. The boss said to take it home, bring back the pie tin tomorrow." He slid the paper out from in front of my father and set the pie in its place.

31

A WEEK BEFORE CHRISTMAS a hot wind began to blow from the east. Santa Ana wind, Mrs. Evola called it. Dust swirled up from the orange groves, papers whipped along Ocean Avenue, and it got hot. It was strange to see Christmas decorations in sun-baked store windows. All along Wiltshire Boulevard in Los Angeles, the trolley standards were wrapped with tinfoil. In the bright sunlight they gave off a fierce glare.

There was a smiling Santa in Bullock's department store in Santa Monica, his face shining with sweat. Fake snow was drifted in the windows, but outside the pavement was hot and bare.

Larry bought a small aluminum Christmas tree that we assembled and put on the table. My father said it fit perfectly.

"A thousand years from now, archaeologists are going to find this thing and they're going to conclude that we lived in a two-dimensional world. Which, in my opinion, is exactly what Los Angeles is. There's no substance here, Larry. It's all flash and glitter. It's like a giant movie screen with people moving around playing at being people, but nothing is real."

"You just say that because you spend your day at the track. I'm real, the people at the diner are real, Tommy is real. What about your friend, Bunny?" He turned to me, "His family is real, isn't it?"

"Sure," I said. "They're from Oklahoma. His dad is a rigger on Signal Hill. His mother makes white gravy that she pours over everything, even pork chops."

"That," Larry said, "is as real as anything gets in this world."

What was unsaid was the fact that all of our spare money was being saved in our City of Hope fund. It had grown to over two hundred dollars, according to Larry. Christmas presents seemed unlikely, and I carefully refrained from mentioning them. I found a ring with a green stone in my scoop, but when I showed it to Mrs. Evola, she said it wasn't worth anything. It was just a piece of dime-store costume jewelry and I hadn't hit the jackpot. Still, I thought I could wrap it in tissue and give it to Larry. My father was particular about his clothes, and kept his shoes shined, neatly placed on the floor, side by side in the evening. I hit upon the idea of making him a pair of shoe trees to stick inside his shoes. I had seen them in an expensive men's store on Santa Monica Boulevard, and I went back several times to memorize their shape. I found two pieces of driftwood on the beach that had been rounded into smooth ovals by the wind and water, and I spent hours in Mrs. Evola's backyard sanding them to fit inside my shoes. I rubbed them with brown shoe polish until they shone like the lacquered ones I had seen in the store.

Christmas morning I got up early to place my gifts under the metal tree. There were two boxes, wrapped in bright paper with my name on them, one of them no bigger than the back of my hand. I was astounded.

Larry and my father were up shortly and Larry made a big deal over the ring—put it on his little finger and held his hand out, turning it this way and that; but I realized right away that he would never wear it. It didn't look like a man's ring on his square hand.

My father, once I had explained what the two pieces of wood were for, said they were just what he needed and he put them into his shoes. My tiny package turned out to be a Westclox wristwatch with an expandable strap. The bigger package was a set of three books: *A Yankee Flyer in North Africa*, *A Yankee Flyer Joins the RAF* and *A Yankee Flyer in the South Pacific*. The South Pacific one still had a dust jacket on it that showed a P-38 diving down on a Japanese Zero over a green island ringed with turquoise water. The other two no longer had dust jackets. We went to Spencer's Snack Shop for Christmas dinner and

had sliced turkey with mashed potatoes and gravy. It was a very satisfactory Christmas.

New Years came and four girls posed for a photographer on the
beach opposite the house in bathing suits, shivering in the January
wind, the low surf behind them. The next day they were on the front
of the *Los Angeles Daily News*, looking as if they were frolicking under
a tropical sun, holding up the numbers 1946. I would turn thirteen this
year, my father would get well, and I resolved to go to school.

I actually tried going back. I showed up at the school office the
next Monday, telling the secretary that we had returned from Arizona,
that my father was cured, and that I wanted to re-enroll.

"You'll have to bring your parents in with you," she said.

"But my father works and my mother is dead," I said. "Besides, I
was already enrolled here last year. You can look it up."

"Rules are rules," she said. "I'm sure your father can get time off to
spend a few minutes in here enrolling you. I suppose he did that the
last time you enrolled, didn't he?" She looked at me over the top of her
glasses.

I tried another tack. "Can I get started today and have him come
in as soon as he gets time off?"

"I don't think that's a good idea," she replied, She handed me a
form. "Why don't you take this home and have him fill it out and sign
it this evening. You can start tomorrow and he can come in as soon as
he gets the time off. How's that?"

It was as good as I was going to get. I thought I could fill out the
form and sign his name to it, but the form asked for things I didn't
know. The kinds and dates of my vaccinations were beyond me. I could
make them up, but if they compared it with my original enrollment,
they wouldn't match. I debated whether or not to attempt the forgery
and decided against it. But I promised myself that I would spend time
in the public library reading, and that I would study the way I had with
Mrs. Green. I would become self-educated, like Abraham Lincoln

32

IT WAS TOO COLD and wet to stay out. Larry had left for work and my father had left for the track. The beach was barely visible in the grayness that filled the spaces, blotting out the Pacific. The trolley tracks on Ocean Avenue shone wetly. The Pier was deserted, the top of the roller coaster disappearing vaguely into the fog that drifted through the timbers. Larry was at work by now and my father would be somewhere on a Red Car east of Los Angeles. The sun would be shining weakly at Santa Anita but here it was clammy, the rides were closed, and only a few concession stands were open with workers idly drinking coffee. An occasional sailor hunched over a counter, wrapped in a thick wool pea coat.

I went back to the apartment and let myself in. I didn't move around much, afraid that Mrs. Evola would find me there in case she thought a stranger had broken in, although why anyone would climb to the attic of a nondescript boarding house certainly hadn't occurred to me.

I read for a while, waiting for the fog to burn off, but it didn't, and in my boredom I went into their bedroom. I sifted through the dresser drawers, looking for anything that might add light to Larry, but there was nothing: no photographs, no diary, only clothes that were familiar. Folded in tissue paper was the blue Navajo shirt I had seen him wear once in the cottage at Metzenbaum's, but had never seen him wear since. When I unfolded the tissue to get a better look at it, I found the ring I had given him at Christmas nestled on top of the bright blue cloth.

In the little closet they shared that was tucked under the slanting eave, I found the leather jacket with the fringe on the shoulders and sleeves and his cowboy boots. His nurse's jacket hung next to the fringed jacket, the tiny enameled pin on the collar. It was a red shield like a miniature knight's shield except this one had a band at the bottom with the words St. Mary's Hospital and the initials RN. Next to it were the red heart and the tiny silver dinosaur pin that I remembered. I don't know what else I expected. It was as if Larry had no past or had carefully erased his past so that whatever had gone on before each moment would not count against him.

In the top drawer of the dresser with my father's neatly folded handkerchiefs I found a little packet of post cards and photographs. I slipped off the rubber band. There was a postcard addressed to my father at an address in Iron Valley, a town in Illinois I had never heard of. The picture on one side showed the Lexington, Kentucky, YWCA and on the other side the words MISSING YOU with a series of big X's across the bottom and a lipstick imprint.

There was a strip of photographs of my mother and sister taken when Pamela was a baby, one of those photo-booth series. In the first one, both of them looked startled. My mother mugged in the other two, but my sister remained in the same position, owl-eyed and solemn.

I found another photograph. It was a picture of my father standing, my mother sitting with me on her lap. At least I assumed it was me. My sister apparently wasn't born yet. Standing behind my mother was an older man. He had one hand on her shoulder and one hand on my father. Was this my grandfather who had used his belt on my father when he was my age? He was jowly, unlike my lean father. But he had the same look, wore the same white shirt, starched, the collar open as if they both had just taken off their ties, except that the older man's sleeves were rolled up and I could see that despite his age, his forearms were beefy and that he was thick-set in the chest.

I searched the photograph for clues to where it might have been taken, but it offered none. In the background was the clapboard wall of a house, plain, with no shrubs or trees. My mother was sitting in what looked like a kitchen chair, perhaps brought outside for the photograph. Who was taking this picture? And why hadn't I known about this grandfather? Was he still alive? Did I have a grandmother somewhere? I had a dim memory of an older woman who must have lived with us when I was very tiny, and who slept in a bed with a feather mattress. She was a big woman and the mattress folded around her when she slept, and I had this faint recollection of trying to sleep with her, rolling down next to her warm body; but when I tried to make the memory more clear, it drew away from me, dissolving.

33

I WENT TO SANTA ANITA for the first time on a Saturday with my father. There was a huge dirt parking lot in front of the track, with an immense grandstand rising on the far side of it, and inside there were a restaurant, several bars, a long room lined on both sides with barred tellers' windows, a clubhouse with tables looking out over the track and waiters who scurried about bringing drinks and food. It was unlike anything I had imagined. I thought it would be just a big oval track with a grandstand, like Arlington Park, which I had seen only when it was empty.

The pictures I had seen in the paper always showed people standing in a bunch along the rail while the horses flew past. Looking across the track from the grandstand, I could see the San Gabriel Mountains, green now that the rains had come.

I went to the clubhouse with my father and he introduced me to some of the men and bought me a Coke.

"Do I have to stay here?" I asked.

"No, you can look around. But when they call the last race, I want you here. You understand?"

At the entrance to the grandstand was the paddock, a small oval where the horses paraded before each race, the jockeys holding the tiny saddles, dressed in brilliant silks, owners and trainers talking and gesturing. Then the jockeys mounted, walked the horses through a tunnel in the grandstand and came out onto the track. There was a bugler in a red hunting outfit who blew the call to the race.

The afternoon sun slanted through long horizontal openings high in the back of the cavernous grandstand. The shadow caused by the grandstand meant that the horses came out of the sun into the darkness, then grew larger as they raced for the finish, the jockeys high in the stirrups flailing with their whips, the hoofs pounding the soft earth and people around me shouting, urging them on. I stood as close as I could to the finish line, astonished at the speed and power that the tiny men, nearly standing on the backs of the horses, seemed to control.

It wasn't until the third or fourth race that I realized that some of them were boys, or at least looked like boys not much older than me. I found my way into the stables, and wandered down the long rows of the low-slung barns, where horses munched and stamped and exercise boys walked horses covered with long blankets. When the call came for the last race I reluctantly returned to the paddock and then to the clubhouse where I waited at a table in the corner while the room emptied out.

"It'll be a few more minutes," my father said. "We have to tally out."

When I asked what that meant, he replied that they had to account for all of their bets—what they had taken in and paid out had to match right down to the penny before anyone could go home. "Sometimes it takes a little longer. The cage tellers are the ones who slow things down. We'll be out of here in half an hour."

On the way home he asked me how I had liked the track. I waxed effusive, describing the stables, the paddock, how I had seen Johnny Longden up close, and even George Jessel. He had appeared just before the last race, wearing a white linen suit and a striped silky tie with a blonde who had hair piled high on her head and lipstick so red it looked like her lips were painted with enamel. He had come through the paddock crowd, and it had parted as if he had an invisible plow blade in front of him, paying no attention to the buzzing voices.

"I saw him the first day I came to the track," my father said. "One of his horses ran in the fourth race."

"Did he win?"

"I don't know. I don't pay much attention to who owns what. The serious bettors don't care much, either. They pay more attention to who the horse's father and mother were."

"They call them sires and dams, don't they?"

"That's right. You pick things up pretty quickly, don't you?"

"It's really great. I want to come out here again."

"I suppose you can," he said. "Maybe next Saturday."

But I wasn't content to wait until Saturday. The only problem was that he worked there, and I knew that I couldn't go near the club-house or be in the grandstand where he might see me. I left for school Monday morning, but I took the Red Car straight downtown, then transferred to the Glendale line that dropped me off at the racetrack. I figured that if I could be at the track long before he got there and left before the day's races were over, there was little chance of being spotted. And I'd spend my time in the stables. They were far more interesting.

I discovered that the horses were still working out when I arrived, and had been on the track since daybreak. At the far end of the track near the stables, trainers on horses bunched against the rail, talking to jockeys who wore plain shirts and old jackets instead of their racing silks, and steam rose from the horses' flanks in the chill morning air. By the time I got there the sun was on the track, the San Gabriels lighting up like brilliant green loaves of bread piled against each other.

I found the jockey school in one of the barns. There, boys my age were practicing on saddles tied to hay bales, learning to stand up and hold their position. They were mostly exercise riders who got to work the horses out in the morning, and I envied them. I wanted to join the jockey school, but when I approached an older man, he asked how long I had been riding.

"Not long," I lied. He burst out laughing.

"How old are you?"

"Fourteen," I lied again.

"You're a big kid," he said. "A couple of years from now you'll be too big to be a jock."

Late in the morning was best. The workouts had ended, horses were being groomed, stables mucked out, and preparations for the afternoon racing began. Birds screeched in the trees that shaded the straw-strewn avenues between the barns, swooping down for spilled grain. If I couldn't be a jockey, then maybe I would learn how to train horses. I'd be one of those men in the paddock surrounded by rich movie stars.

I learned to read the tote board, what odds were, how much the horses paid, what place and show meant. I began reading the racing section of the newspaper when Larry brought it home from the diner each evening. I asked my father on a Saturday trip to the track if he could place a bet for me.

"I can't do that," he said.

"If I give it to someone in the clubhouse, would they do it?"

"Where would you get the money?"

"It's from my beachcombing. I just want to try it once."

"It's a foolish idea, Tommy."

I had eavesdropped enough in the stables to know when a horse was moving in class, the kind of thing that regulars would know, but the casual bettor wouldn't. But I didn't dare let my father know how much I knew.

"There's a horse I'd like to bet on," I said.

"What horse?"

"Sweet Victory. Fred Astaire owns him."

"How do you know about this Sweet Victory?"

"I read the papers every night. You've seen me. Can't I, just this once?"

I sat next to a man I had come to know on my Saturday visits and he smiled when I asked him if he'd place a two-dollar bet for me."

"Your father know you're playing the nags?" he asked as I held out two one-dollar bills.

"Sort of," I said. "He said I could do it just this once."

Sweet Victory went off at 10-1 and suddenly I was twenty dollars richer.

"Jeez, kid, maybe you should bet for me," the man said when he slipped me the payoff.

That night my father could hardly contain himself when Larry got home.

"Guess what Tommy did today."

"I have no idea," Larry said. He looked tired.

"He placed a two-dollar bet at the track and won twenty dollars!"

"Eddie, kids can't place bets. Did you book it for him?"

"No, one of the regulars did. I had no idea." He paused and looked at me. "Although I think I should have known. He was pestering me on the way to the track to do it. But I had no idea he'd actually lay down a bet."

Larry didn't seem pleased.

"I suppose so," he said. "So what are you going to do with your twenty bucks?"

"I'm putting it with the City of Hope money."

"Jesus Christ, Eddie," he said, hanging his coat over the back of a chair. "I don't think you've got a clue."

34

"YOU GOT TO REMEMBER a couple of things," Mrs. Evola said. She stood in the back yard feeding trash into the oil drum incinerator. "People are gonna tell you if you build a fire on the beach it keeps them from coming in. That's not so. They'll come in anyway, no matter what. But when they're ready, you can see them out there in that wave all squirming and squishing together so they look like foam in the water. A few of them come out of the first wave, flopping by themselves on the wet sand, just a couple of them. Somebody is going to want to run and grab those first ones. Folks say those first ones are some kind of scouts, and if you grab them, the others are going to stay back; they won't come in to lay their eggs. Of course that ain't true, neither. But there's no point in grabbing those anyway. You want to wait. In that next wave, or maybe the one after that, they're going to come. They'll slide up the sand like they was the water."

She had her hands spread out now, flat, sliding back and forth as she spoke.

"Oh boy, there's gonna be so many of them it's gonna look like somebody threw a silver sheet on the beach, all shiny and wiggling. You wait and see. And then everybody goes nuts, folks rushing into the water, scooping them up, and those little fishies doing what they came to do. What with the moon and the fires on the beach and folks yelling and the fish coming out of the sea, you won't forget it."

The cars began to arrive in late afternoon. More and more people got off the trolleys. They had blankets, coats, buckets, sacks of wood, crates, Coleman lanterns and picnic hampers. By six o'clock it was nearly dark and cars were parked bumper to bumper all along the street. The beach had people all over it, like it was a Saturday afternoon.

We had supper and watched out the window. In the dark, fires glowed as far down the beach as I could see. There was noise from the street. The rumble of the street cars, normally forgotten, was now pronounced; there were knots of people around the fires on the beach, and more and more people came down the street, climbing down the steps to the sand.

I wanted to go down on the beach but Larry said there was no point in going yet. The *Times* said the high tide wasn't going to come until after midnight. There had been a picture in the *Times* of a grunion run from the past, the white faces of people caught in the flash of the photographer, scooping up fish with their hands into overflowing buckets.

You couldn't use nets, Mrs. Evola said, but you could use anything else. Men used shirts; women used their skirts, hands, cans, buckets.

By ten o'clock, it got too much for me.

"All right," my father said, "you can go down, but come back up here so you can go down with us. I want you back here in an hour."

I wandered down the beach, keeping in the darkness between the fires, seeing faces glowing red, men drinking beer, some groups toasting marshmallows and hot dogs over the flames, others with buckets lined up; some were setting up grills and pans as if this were a giant cookout. It was cold now. I went close to the water and looked out, half-expecting, I think, to see the fish waiting the way the people were waiting, gathered in knots, anticipating the rush to the shore. There was a strange phosphorescence to the waves. The moon was up now: big, cold, pure white. When I looked back down the beach, the Pier seemed other-worldly, shining a dull bluish silver. There were lights on along the boulevard, yellow lights in the streetcars that rumbled past.

I went back up to the apartment. Larry was busy assembling things. He had the dish pan, two large coffee cans and a pail he used for mopping the floor.

"Are we going to keep them?" my father asked. "I thought we were just going down to watch."

"Why not? Larry answered. "They're supposed to be good. And they're free. You want to, don't you, Sport?"

I nodded my head.

At eleven-thirty we went downstairs, across the street and down the steps to the beach. It was even more crowded now, people moving toward the hiss and thump of the dark water. The surf was low, no more than a line of foot-tall waves that flopped on the beach and receded. A great wave of people with buckets and cans had gathered along the sloping sand, rising up, waiting to topple forward into the flattened sea.

We came up behind the advancing line. My father held back.

"You wait here, Eddie," Larry said. He spread a blanket on the sand.

"Here." He handed me the dishpan and an empty coffee can, taking the bucket and the other can for himself.

Leaning one hand on my shoulder, he took off one shoe, dropped it on the blanket, then took off the other.

"Take your shoes off," he said. He rolled his trouser cuffs up to his knees, then hitched them higher, leaving his pale legs exposed.

The waves were farther up the sand now, the edge of the water sliding in a long sheet that almost touched the line of people. A few voices shouted out in the dark, but mostly it was quiet. Then, in the light of the moon, I saw the first fish dancing free at the edge of the water, just the way our landlady had said they would, as if it were on a hot skillet dancing and flapping. A cry went up and down the beach, a great yelling and cheering. On the next wave a few more fish flopped free and one or two people dashed for them, grabbing at their slippery bodies. There were more yells, and suddenly, with the next wave, there was a shimmering, slippery, silvery foam that spilled out of the face of the wave and rushed up the beach, wriggling and flapping. I was transfixed. People rushed into the water, falling to their hands and knees, slapping and grabbing at the tiny things as the water receded, women scooping with their skirts, throwing the fish into buckets.

Larry and I rushed forward. The fish were everywhere. Some of them were upended, as if they were dancing on their tails, drilling down into the soft wet sand right at the edge of the water, sliding into holes that their tails had scoured, surrounded immediately by wriggling fish five or six inches long. In the moonlight and the light of the fires on the beach and the Coleman lanterns, they sparkled like jewels. Up and down the beach, the water's edge was filled with a scrambling mass of people and fish, the fish glinting as far as I could see, disappearing into the blackness of the ocean. Grunion were all around me, moving so that I felt unbalanced. The earth trembled, I grabbed at them, and they slipped from my hands. I turned the can on its side and slapped them into it, emptying it as fast as I could into the dishpan.

They flapped and bounced. In a few minutes the pan was half full. With each succeeding wave more came, and the ones that were on the beach slid back into the water; and then, as if someone had turned off a faucet, the next wave had fewer fish, and there were only one or two here and there. A great sigh went up along the beach. A few fish flopped on the sand out of reach of the next wave, and I realized the fish had come in on the half-dozen waves that had reached the farthest, timing their return perfectly, and now they had rushed back into the sea to whatever watery lives they lived.

People trudged back up the beach with pails of fish. Cars started on the street; frying fish mixed with the sea smell of kelp and salt air.

We sat on the blanket next to my father and Larry and I dried our feet and legs with a towel. Larry leaned back, his head across my father's lap and his hands folded across his chest. I could barely see them in the darkness.

"Well," my father said, "I don't think we need to give Tommy any speeches about the birds and the bees after this scene."

"Eddie!" Larry said in mock surprise. "We were just catching our dinner."

"Like hell you were." There was a silence and I became conscious of the glow of the fires, the echoing of voices along the beach and the soft thump of the surf. Then my father spoke again, but his voice had changed.

"Goddammit," was all he said, but I knew immediately what had happened. He was disconnected from the life of the beach, a sick man on a blanket surrounded by passionate people, like a ghost who, when he tries to touch the life that surrounds him, finds to his dismay that his fingers have no feeling. I suddenly thought of the headless lady in the freak show at Long Beach and I wanted to touch him, but Larry lay on his lap, reaching up a shadowy hand to touch my father's face while I sat, miles away on the other end of the blanket in the darkness. I was angry at Larry who had slipped into our lives in a way I could not understand but somehow knew was at odds with the rest of the world, and at Dr. Metzenbaum who had not cured my father, and at my mother who had abandoned us, and at the upside-down edge of the continent where winter was summer and fish came out of the water to dance on the sand. I, too, wanted to yell "Goddammit!" but at that moment the world seemed too busy with itself to care much about me.

Larry sat up.

"Come on," he said, wrapping our shoes in the towel. He reached out and took my father's hand, pulling him to his feet. Larry and I shook out the blanket and he draped it over my father's shoulders. We took our cans and fish and headed for the lights of Ocean Avenue. It was slow going in the soft dry sand and my father was a few steps ahead when I looked at him, round-shouldered, clutching the bunched cloth at his throat, a fragile figure in his blanket cloak, silhouetted by the street lights above and ahead of us.

Our apartment seemed bright after the darkness of the beach, the lights so hard and yellow that my eyes ached. My father went into their little bedroom and lay on the bed, leaving the door open. Larry spilled the fish into the sink. He ran water over the silver clot, washing off the slippery mucous that coated them.

"How do you clean them?" I asked.

"We don't. Just fry them up and eat them, according to Mrs. Evola. The bones get soft and everything gets cooked."

Apparently Larry had been talking to our landlady about grunion, too. He placed a frying pan on the hot plate, put several lumps of white margarine in to melt, and poured some flour into an old paper bag. He shook salt and pepper into it, dropped a handful of the tiny fish in the bag and shook it. Then he dropped each white-coated fish into the hot fat. They sizzled, turning golden brown, their eyes immediately clouding over. The smell of hot oil and flour and salt and pepper filled the room. I saw my mother standing at the stove in Chicago frying chicken on a Sunday afternoon. It was the first time I had thought of her that way in a long time, and I felt a lump fill my chest so that I either had to cry out or sob. I yelled, "Wow! What a night!" startling Larry and causing my father to call out from the bedroom, "What's going on out there?"

"Nothing. Tommy's having some sort of a fit."

He laid the hot fish on a sheet of newspaper to drain and arched his eyebrows.

"You okay?" he asked.

The lump was dissolving and the woman at the frying pan was Larry again.

35

AT BREAKFAST SATURDAY MORNING my father had an announcement: "We're all going to the races."

He had the little wooden box where they kept the City of Hope money in front of him on the table.

"Santa Anita Handicap today," he said. "And we're going to bet on a horse."

He opened the box and laid the money on the table..

"Eddie, have you gone out of your mind?" Larry asked.

I had a sinking feeling.

My father began to count the money, placing the ones, tens and twenties in separate piles. "Two hundred and thirty-one dollars," he said. He took a single dollar bill off the top of one pile and placed it in the box. "Seed money," he said, and closed the box.

"Eddie," Larry persisted. "What the hell's going on?"

"All my life," my father said, "I've played it safe. Except when I married Rose and when I came to California with you and when I made book on my own at the track. I was awake half the night thinking about it. So today we're going to bet it all on a horse. What do you think, Sport?" He turned to me.

I had never heard him call me that. I think I assumed he was feverish, or that it was some sort of joke. But he carefully folded the money and put it in his shirt pocket.

"What about the City of Hope? " I asked.

"We're going to roll the dice, Tommy. If we get lucky today, then I check into the City of Hope. If we don't, then I check into the County

Hospital. Come on, you two. You're the big risk-takers. Let's have a little enthusiasm. Today's our lucky day."

His face had the rosy glow of fever that I knew. It looked the way it had that afternoon at Metzenbaum's when he had talked about the dangerous place with the French name.

"Jesus, Eddie," Larry said.

"Santa Anita Handicap," my father said. "Fourth time is the charm."

We caught the express car for Los Angeles. I still didn't believe that we were going to bet all of the City of Hope savings on a horse race, but my father had the sports page and we studied it as the car sped through soggy orange groves, past puddled streets, the pale February sun coming out for the first time in a week. Larry didn't know much about the races, and my father explained how they were handicapped. I knew Johnny Longden usually rode horses owned by Louis B. Mayer and that he won nearly a million dollars the year before. There was a $100,000 prize for winning the 'Cap and if we were going to bet the money, I thought we should bet on a horse that Longden would ride.

"No," my father said. "He'll go off at not much more than even money. You bet two hundred dollars on him and get back two hundred and ten. There's no point in doing this unless we bet on a long shot."

"But you said long shots were dumb bets."

"Not that long a shot," he replied.

This was not my father talking.

"Look," Larry said. "Here's a horse called Paperboy. He's eleven to one. And the jockey's name is Bill Bailey. That's one of our favorite songs. 'Won't you come home, Bill Bailey, won't you come home,'" he sang, loud enough so that several passengers turned to look at us. "And Tommy has a paper route. That makes him a paperboy."

I wanted to tell him that I had lied, that I never had a paper route, that I hadn't gone to school, and that he wanted to throw all our money away on a dumb horse ridden by some dumb guy who didn't have a chance against horses owned by Hollywood movie stars and ridden by Johnny Longden and Ted Atkinson.

To my astonishment, my father said, "Not a bad choice, Larry. What do you say, Sport?"

I wanted to yell at him to stop calling me Sport, but I didn't say anything, just sat there dumbly while we rattled across the Los Angeles basin.

Paperboy was listed on the tote board at 15-1 and my father bet the whole two hundred and thirty dollars on him. He gave the ticket to Larry to hold "for luck," he said, but Larry said we should all three hold it, so we clasped hands, mine inside my father's, Larry's large hand holding both of ours, the ticket buried in my clenched palm. I wondered what Bunny's father would say if he saw the three of us holding hands, my body pressed between the two men who were, as near as I could tell, now both my parents.

We stood at the rail, looking out across the infield toward the San Gabriel Mountains, the long shadow of the grandstand stretching across the track, darkening the tote board in the center. The 'Cap didn't come until the last race of the day, so we rooted for horses, Larry picking names he liked, my father and I looking at the program and trying to handicap them. We would have lost all of our money if we'd actually bet on the horses we picked. I had the sinking feeling that we would lose all of the City of Hope money and my father would go to the County Hospital. I remembered him saying that he would have a better chance betting hundred-to-one shots at the track.

After the eighth race we went to the paddock to watch the horses parade and Paperboy didn't look like anything special. Neither did Bill Bailey. Paperboy shied when Bailey tried to mount him, rolling his eyes at the crowd that pressed to the rail. Finally the trainer threw a blanket over his head so they could get the saddle strapped on and Bailey on top.

"That's good," Larry said. "It shows he wants to run."

"It just shows he's nervous and doesn't like crowds." I said. I knew the City of Hope money was down the drain. My father didn't say anything.

The call to the race came and the outriders grabbed each horse by the bridle as it came to the tunnel, leading them under the grandstand.

"Come on, you two," Larry urged. We worked our way through the crowd, pausing only long enough to look at the board above us where Paperboy's odds hadn't changed. At least he wasn't 100-1, I thought. "Dumb long shots." That's what my father had said. I wondered if 15-1 was long enough to be dumb.

We found a place at the rail near the finish line. The horses were on the track now, some of them walking, others cantering off around the first curve. They would go all the way around to the bottom of the backstretch where the gate was waiting. Paperboy was galloping full out, overtaking other horses.

"Look," Larry said. "He's really full of it. Oh, I know he's going to win."

I looked at my father but he had his arm around Larry's shoulder and he was smiling as if Larry had said the most brilliant thing in the world.

It was apparent that Paperboy would be too tired in the stretch if the dumb jockey didn't pull him up. Dumb seemed to be the only word I knew that afternoon. Paperboy was first at the gate, first in, then reared several times and had to be backed out. Finally they were all in, the crowd hushed, there was the clanging bell that we could hear all the way across the track and the loudspeakers echoed, "They're off!"

The first time they went by, Paperboy was in the middle of the field, jammed against the rail. I didn't want to look. They began to spread out on the backstretch and rounding the backstretch turn it was hard to see who was ahead. They came out of the final turn, the leaders four abreast, the rest of the field trailing, the jockeys riding high, whips flailing and the yellow silks of Bill Bailey were on one of the horse we could see.

Then the horses were by in a pounding rush, the crowd roaring and Bill Bailey in his yellow silks was standing in the stirrups, waving his whip in triumph. Paperboy didn't quit running until the top of the backstretch.

We stood there, stunned. Larry grabbed my father and began dancing him round and round. "How much have we won?" he kept asking and my father repeated, "Three thousand four hundred and fifty dollars."

Larry reached out to include me in his embrace. "Oh, sweet Jesus," he said and then he burst out singing, "Won't you come home, Bill Bailey" at the top of his lungs and railbirds around us all cheered. We went to the window together and watched while the teller counted out the money.

"I never had a paper route," I told my father as we walked toward the Red Car stop. "I lied about it."

"That's a talent of yours that you're going to have to learn how to use a bit more constructively," he said, squeezing his arm around my shoulder. "Maybe when you grow up you can sell orange grove lots to farmers from Iowa."

36

SUNDAY MORNING THE THREE of us celebrated by going to the Boardwalk at Ocean Park Pier. We ate Belgian waffles with real maple syrup at a restaurant. Applying Bunny's advice at the shooting gallery, I won a blue felt pennant that had "The Golden State" on it in gold letters which I promptly presented to Larry. He and I rode the bumper cars while my father watched, and we had our pictures taken by a man who had a portrait camera on a tripod. He took a picture of the three of us together, one of Larry and my father and a third one of my father with his arm around my shoulder. I was almost as tall as he was. That afternoon we rented an umbrella and chairs and sat watching the waves. Several times that afternoon either my father or Larry would reach out to touch the other's hand. It made me feel better to know that Larry cared for my father as much as I did. I was no longer angry with him. There was no doubt that we were rich.

My father didn't get up early the next day. He said he was worn out from the excitement of the weekend. The track was closed Monday and Tuesday, and he said he would call Wednesday and tell them he was quitting. I made no pretense to leave the apartment and Larry said nothing before he left for work. My father remained in their little bedroom.

I read for a while in the last of the Yankee Flyer books, then quietly went to the door of his room. It was open and I could see him lying on the bed in his white sleeveless undershirt. He had on his gabardine trousers, as if he had begun to dress for work, but had stopped halfway. His skin was as white as the ribbed cotton under-shirt. In the background I could hear the whispering undertone of the traffic and the rush of the ocean. His skin looked soft and his chest was concave. It barely rose and fell as he breathed. I stood in the doorway looking at him. Sensing I was there, he turned his head so he could see me.

"You didn't go to school?"

"Not today. I thought I'd stick around in case you need anything."

"I don't think I will, but it's a good thought. How's school going?"

"Okay. I should be in seventh grade, though. The stuff we do is too easy."

"When I get better, I'll go and talk to them. See about moving you."

"When are you going to the City of Hope?"

"Soon, I hope. I'm on the waiting list. We've got more than enough money now."

"Are you getting worse?"

"It comes and goes, Tommy. Don't worry. This is just a bad day. What I need is a bit of sleep." He closed his eyes.

I went back to my bed by the front window and read for a while, but every few minutes I got up, tip-toed to his door, and looked in. I waited until I could see the rising and falling of his chest before going back to my book. I had read in a book of Greek mythology about the twin brothers, Sleep and Death. Running through my head was the only prayer I knew: "Now I lay me down to sleep. I pray the Lord my soul to keep. If I should die before I wake, I pray the Lord my soul to take." Each time I stopped at the line "If I should die before I wake." There were two frightening brothers, identical in every way, coming to place their hands over your eyes and you drifted off, but you never knew which brother was going to close your eyelids. And, if by chance, it was Death, you didn't wake. The Lord kept your soul. Perhaps, I thought that day, if I stayed awake, my father wouldn't die. As long as I could keep my eyes open while his were closed, I could keep the wrong brother from laying his smooth hand on my father's eyelids. It sounds stupid, but I read every word in *A Yankee Flyer in the South Pacific* out loud in a quiet voice, making sure I didn't drift off there on my bed facing the Pacific Ocean.

I wanted my father once again to be the man with the hat in his white shirtsleeves, standing on the grass in the park, Lake Michigan glinting in the sun behind him.

My father was up and at the table for dinner that night, his forehead shining with sweat, but insisting that he felt fine. We had macaroni and cheese, a staple in our little household, something Larry could easily cook on the hot plate. For dessert we had the remains of a pie that Larry had, as he put it, "liberated" from the snack shop.

I tried staying awake that night after they went to bed. For a while I could hear their voices, Larry's voice insistent, my father's voice reasoned, calm. Then they were silent. I watched the streetcars going by on Ocean Avenue, yellow light spilling out on the pavement, sparks dripping from the overhead wires. The cars stopped running at midnight and I fell asleep. When I woke, my father was dressed.

"Come on, sleepyhead, get up. You'll be late for school." He was shaved and ready for work, as if yesterday hadn't happened. "I'll walk you to school today. How's that?"

"No, I can go by myself," I said, suddenly panicked.

"Don't want to be embarrassed by your old man?"

"Something like that. I mean, you don't embarrass me or anything, but parents don't walk their kids—you know. . ."

"Okay," he said. "Come on. Time to get a move on. Larry's still in bed. He works the late shift tonight. I'll see you at supper time."

"Are you going to the City of Hope?"

"No, I have to go into Los Angeles for an appointment."

But I didn't see him that evening.

I took the Red Car to Griffith Park and then, in the afternoon went to Willowbrook where I waited for Bunny to come out after school. We worked in his back yard on a fort he was building out of orange crates we had found in back of a neighborhood market.

"I don't go to school," I said.

"You mean not ever?" He looked incredulous, but Bunny always looked that way.

"No. I just don't go."

"What does your dad say?"

"He doesn't know."

"Jeez, he must be pretty dumb."

"No. but he's pretty sick."

"What do you mean, sick?"

"Do you know what tuberculosis is?"

Bunny stopped puling the wire out of an orange crate. "No. What is it?"

"It's a disease people get in their lungs. Sometime they get it in their bones, too, but mostly it's in their lungs. It eats away at them and a lot of times they die."

"Is your dad dying?"

"I don't know. Sometimes I think so. Like yesterday. But today he seems okay."

"How come you never told me this before?"

"Tuberculosis scares a lot of people. They think they're going to get it if they hang around someone who's near it."

"Can I get it from you?"

"No. You might get it from my dad, though. That's why I never invited you to my house."

"How come you're telling me now?"

"I guess I had to tell somebody. You're my best friend. But he's going to get well. He's going to a special hospital in Arcadia where they can cure him. We won $3,500 at Santa Anita betting on a horse Saturday and now he can afford this special drug they have."

"Your father won $3500 on a horse race? I don't believe that."

"It's true. All three of us bet on it—my dad, my uncle Larry, and me. The horse was named Paperboy. You can look it up in the paper."

"It won't say if you won, though."

"It's the truth. Cross my heart."

Mrs. Smith asked if I wanted to stay for supper and I asked if I could telephone Mrs. Evola so she could tell my father I would be home late. We had fried chicken and Bunny's father told stories about a man he worked with that they called Tiny.

"He's the biggest man I ever seen," he said.

"Bigger than the giant at the boardwalk on the Long Beach Pier?" Bunny asked.

"Well, maybe not as tall, but I'll bet anything he weighs more than three hundred pounds. And eat? He eats a whole chicken in his lunch box. I mean he's got hisself a whole chicken in there and a loaf of bread and oranges and potato salad and I don't know what all. How he gets all that stuff what with rationing and all, I'll never know. And he isn't fat, neither. He's all muscle. It's a hard task to keep up with him on the rig."

"I knew an Indian in Arizona named Tiny," I said.

"Is that so?" Mr. Smith forked a mouthful of fried potatoes.

"He was big, too."

"Well, now, isn't that something. And how big was your Indian friend?"

"He was big," I said. "Once he rescued me from a box canyon when I got stuck."

"I bet you're making that up," Bunny said.

"No, I'm not," I said. "There were three Indians I knew. Tiny and the Chief and Willie, only Tiny got beat to death by some men in Williams. I was there."

It had all come out in a rush.

Mr. Smith broke the silence that followed. "I'm sorry to hear that. There are some things in life that just don't offer an explanation."

When I got home, I was surprised to find Larry alone in the apartment.

"I've been worried sick about you," he said.

"Didn't Mrs. Evola tell you where I was?"

"Yes, but you were supposed to be here, not halfway to Los Angeles."

"Where's Dad?"

"Eddie is in the hospital in Los Angeles."

"You mean he's at the City of Hope?"

"No, he's at the county hospital. He went there this morning to see a doctor and they wouldn't let him go."

"Why can't he go to the City of Hope?"

"He's very sick again, Tommy. He had no choice. We'll go see him tomorrow."

"Have you seen him?"

"No. Now don't ask me anything else. I don't know anything else. They called me at the diner from the hospital. That's all I know." He ran his fingers through my hair.

"Don't worry. He'll be all right."

But he wasn't all right. The next morning we took the Red Car downtown to the county hospital, the same low ramshackle collection of wooden buildings where I had my X-ray. We found my father in the isolation ward. He was in a room like the one at Metzenbaum's with a glass partition so that visitors could see patients but not breathe the same air. There were three men in the large room, their beds against the opposite wall. The nurse who attended them wore a white mask over her face.

My father was propped up by pillows and he waved to me, mouthed a "How are you?"

"I'm fine," I said to the glass wall. "Can I go inside?" I asked Larry, who stood next to me, knowing the answer would be no.

"You stay here," Larry said. "I'm going to talk to the doctor."

I watched my father for a while. He smiled and waved again and made pantomime motions as if he were reading a book, then pointed at me. He wanted to know what I was reading. I mimed a baseball pitch, then swung an imaginary bat, as if I were striking at a baseball. He looked puzzled.

"*Strikeout Story*," I mouthed at the window. "About Bob Feller." But he couldn't understand me and his eyebrows went up quizzically. Then he began to cough, grabbed a fistful of tissues and held them to his mouth. I could hear nothing through the glass, but I knew that racking sound, as if his lungs were coming up, his stomach convulsing, shoulders hunched into a ball. The nurse appeared at his side and tried to take the tissues from his face, but he motioned with his other hand at the window. She turned, saw me, and leaned over so that I couldn't see his face. When she leaned back his head was against the pillow, his eyes closed, and I knew that the tissues were spotted with red. I waited until he opened his eyes. He waved feebly at me, managed a smile. I waved back.

37

THAT NIGHT THERE WAS a knock on the door that woke me. Half-awake, I saw that it was Mrs. Evola in a night dress, a bathrobe clutched around her, talking urgently to Larry. Larry put his coat on over his pajamas and closed the door softly. I waited, knowing that whatever it was, at this hour it would not be good news.

When he came back I sat up and asked, "What is it?"

He came to my bed and sat on the edge. "The hospital telephoned. I'm sorry Tommy. Your father passed away."

I don't think I cried. I remember thinking about Metzenbaum's Captain of All These Men of Death and the "galloping consumption" that took victims in a rush. Metzenbaum's Captain had come on horseback while I slept.

Larry and I listened to his records for a while, the volume turned so low I could hear the scratching of the needle in the groove. Then it began to get light outside and Larry said I should try to get some sleep.

"It's not fair!" I said. "We had all the money he needed. They could have cured him at the City of Hope!"

"Fairness has nothing to do with it, Tommy. He was too far gone. I think he knew it when he got up Saturday morning and we went to the races."

"*Merde!*" I said.

"Where did you learn that?"

"From Mrs. Green."

Larry smiled. "I think it's shitty, too, Tommy."

He turned up the volume and put another record on. "Come on, I'm going to teach you to dance." And there, in the early morning light of Mrs. Evola's shabby room, with the Andrews sisters singing softly and the gray Pacific Ocean emerging out of the fog, I learned to dance. Larry held me close and I couldn't see his face, but I knew he was crying.

We held each other for a while after the record ended, and then Larry said he was going to get dressed and make some phone calls. Mrs. Evola had told him he could use the phone.

I went back to bed and fell asleep almost immediately. When I awoke a streetcar was going by outside. It was mid-morning, cars lined the street, and beachgoers were trudging across the sand with their blankets and chairs and picnic boxes.

Larry came back shortly after.

"You okay?" he asked.

"Yes. I guess so. What happens to me now?"

"I tracked down your mother. You're going to live with her and your sister and your grandmother."

"I have a grandmother?"

"Holy Jesus, Mother of God!" Larry exclaimed. "You didn't even know you had a grandmother? I never knew such a family. Nobody ever talked to anybody about anything important!"

"How did you find her?"

"It wasn't hard. Your father had an address in Kentucky. I called information and got her that way."

"Does she want me?"

"Yes. She said to put you on a train." He looked at me for a moment. "Jesus, did you think I was going to put you in an orphanage or something? If worse came to worse, I would have taken you myself. You want to stay in bed or do you want to get up and get some lunch?"

I got up and we took the Red Car to the Snack Shop where we had hamburgers and French fries. The cook said he was sorry to hear about my father and the waitress kept refilling my glass of Coke and asking if I wanted more fries, so I figured they all knew but weren't sure how to deal with me.

Back at the apartment Larry told me he had to make some arrangements. Would I be okay by myself, or would it be better if I went down and stayed with Mrs. Evola? I said I'd be okay in the apartment, and after Larry left I got out my father's little package of cards and photographs and spread them on the table. I got out my beach-combing money and laid it on the table and counted it. I had twelve dollars and thirty-five cents. I looked at the bed where Larry and my father had slept. Larry had carefully made it up. He had a nurse's talent for making beds so tightly that sliding into one was like slipping into an envelope.

My father was not in the bed and he wasn't in a cottage with three other men and he wasn't at the racetrack. He simply wasn't. It was as if there was a space where nothing was. It wasn't a hole. A hole had sides and a bottom and you could fill it with something. I remembered once at Metzenbaum's looking for something in the old encyclopedia that was on the shelf in the patients' dayroom. When I came to the entry, there was a hole cut neatly into the page. I couldn't figure it out, since it didn't seem to conform to the print, but when I turned to the other side of the page, I discovered that someone had cut out the picture of a dog. The entry was there next to the place where the picture had been: border collie. Perhaps some patient, longing for a dog that had been left behind, had cut out the picture. Or perhaps a child had cut out the picture long before the encyclopedia had been given to Metzenbaum. All of the books there had been cast-off gifts or left behind. Unlike whoever had cut out the picture of the dog, I had nothing of my father. He was simply the hole in the page.

There was a small metal box with my father's things, and I opened it. Inside were a marriage license, my birth certificate and a piece of paper with my vaccinations noted in his meticulous hand. There was an Illinois driver's license and a Santa Fe timetable for 1945 with a star next to the train we had come west on. A little address book contained several names I knew: Dr. Metzenbaum; Earl Joyner; there was a woman in Dabney, Kentucky, named Charity Farwell who I assumed must be my grandmother. I looked back at the marriage certificate and my mother's maiden name was Farwell. She, too, was in the book, living at the same address in Dabney as Charity Farwell.

There was a folding map of the United States. Our route to Arizona was traced in red ink and the date of our arrival was next to Williams. Then the red line continued along Route 66 to California, with another arrival date carefully lettered on the edge of the Pacific Ocean.

I thought of Mrs. Green and our geography lessons. I put my finger on Kentucky. It was pale blue. Daniel Boone was from there. They had mountains and bears. Perhaps my grandmother lived in a log cabin.

I don't remember much about the rest of the day. When he came home, Larry asked me where Bunny's family lived, and they arrived the next day, dressed in Sunday clothes, stiff, not knowing what to say. Mrs. Smith had a basket with her with fried chicken wrapped in a dish towel and potatoes and gravy in bowls she heated on the hotplate. Bunny and I finally escaped and ran off to the Pier where we ate salt-water taffy and rode the bumper cars.

I rode back to Willowbrook on the Red Car with the Smiths and stayed with them while Larry made more of what he called "arrangements."

I wished that I could do something like Willie and the Chief had done after Tiny died, but of course burning down Mrs. Evola's house was out of the question. Larry kept waiting for me to cry.

38

LARRY MADE ARRANGEMENTS FOR my father's body to be shipped back to Kentucky on the train. He sent another telegram to my mother and got one back saying they would be waiting for me in Lexington, the nearest stop on the railroad to where they lived. My father would be buried in the same cemetery with my mother's people. By the time Larry had paid for the Pullman ticket for me, given Mrs. Evola the last month's rent, bought me new trousers, shoes, and a jacket for the trip, paid the mortuary, bought a casket for my father, and paid the cost of shipping his body east, we still had more than twenty-five hundred dollars left.

I thought we should split it, but Larry said no, he didn't need more than a hundred dollars to tide him over. He could always get a job nursing if he needed to. I should take the money to my mother.

"Why can't I stay with you?" I asked. We were sitting in Spencer's Snack Shop. It was a boat-shaped diner with silvery aluminum sides, windows all around, and a bright band of neon tubes that circled the low-slung roof. In the glow of the neon, our faces took on a purple hue.

"You're not my kid," he said. "I think you're terrific, but I can't take care of you."

"My mother didn't want me when Dad got sick," I said.

"I think she let your father hold on to something he valued more than anything in this world. Sometimes people get scared, Tommy, and they turn tail and run, and when the smoke clears, they look back and wish they could do it all over again."

The glasses on the mirrored shelf behind the counter glowed in the glare of the headlights of a car that nosed into a parking slot behind us.

"Your friend Bunny's family thinks I'm your uncle. How come?"

"I told them you were my uncle. I said you were my mother's brother."

"Did you tell everyone I was your uncle?"

"Yes."

"Why"

"Because."

"Because it was easier for you?"

"Yes."

"Was I that hard to explain?"

"You weren't hard to explain. It seemed like you were related to us."

"There were times when I felt like it. But it was more than that. Some day, Tommy, maybe you'll understand."

"I understand that you liked my dad an awful lot. More than if you were brothers."

"I'm not your uncle."

"I know it."

"I never was your uncle."

"I know that, too."

"I think you know a great deal, Tom Hall."

He had always called me Sport or Tommy or, when he was talking to my father, 'your kid, Eddie.' This was the first time he had called me by a grown-up name.

"I think you know things that some people my age never learn."

He stopped talking and looked at me. It couldn't have been for more than a few seconds, but I was uncomfortable, as if he were looking inside me for one of those things, or perhaps offering me a chance to see something inside him.

"Jesus!" he suddenly exclaimed, and it startled me. He reached out and yanked me toward him. I thought I was going to fall off the stool, but he only tousled my hair and spun me around on the stool and then said, "You want another hamburger? Charlie will make you one." The cook, lounging behind the counter at his grill, nodded.

"No, I'm full."

"You never went to school, did you?"

"No. I don't know why. I like school."

"When you get to Kentucky, you'll go to school, won't you?"

I nodded.

"I wish I could stay with you," I told him.

"Damn it, Tom, don't start that again."

"You ever going to come and visit me?"

"Probably not. When you're older, maybe you'll come and see me."

"There was a girl at Metzenbaum's who told me to come back and see her in six years."

"Was she pretty?"

"It was Opal, but she had a boyfriend."

Larry smiled. "Six years is a long time. Hell, six months is a long time."

The counter and the booths were filling up. Charlie was sweating at the grill, calling out orders, the waitress moved back and forth in her white uniform.

"You could use your nurse's uniform here," I said.

Larry laughed. "Big night," he said. "What's up, Charlie?"

"George Jessel's opening a movie at the theater down the street. Big deal."

"I saw George Jessel at the race track," I said.

"Really?" Larry took some money from his wallet and laid it on the counter.

"Come on. Unlike you and Eddie, I've never seen a movie star."

There was a Fox theater two blocks away, and the traffic had stacked up all around it. Spotlights out in front roamed back and forth in the foggy night, their motors humming, the arcs spitting out a high-pitched buzz. Short slashes of light flashed back and forth, dissolving into the gray just above the theater. On the marquee were block letters: GEORGE JESSEL STARS IN PERSON 8:30. Flags and bunting hung down from the roof and a rope was stretched across the sidewalk in front of the theater with people clustered at either end. Policemen, the bills of their blue-black caps damp from the wetness of the night, stood in the street, directing traffic. We stood across the street for a while, watching cars stop and unload. 8:30 came and went, the crowd thinned out, and we hadn't seen George Jessel.

"Maybe he was inside when we got here." I said. I wished Larry had seen him.

On the way home in the streetcar, Larry turned to me. "Don't you ever feel like crying, Tom? Or do you do your crying when I can't see it?"

"Not much," I said. "I guess too many people died on me this year. It seems like everywhere I went, people I liked died. Not you, of course, or Bunny. Or Mrs. Evola. But it wasn't just old people. Tiny wasn't old and dad wasn't old. And Mrs. Green didn't seem old. But one day they were here and the next day they were gone."

Larry put his arm around me and pulled me close. He smelled of soap and some sort of cologne.

"What's that smell you have?" I asked.

"Lavender. Your dad liked it. He said it reminded him of lilacs."

We didn't talk after that, just watched out the window at the reflection of the streetcar lights on the wet pavement like a lighted cardboard cutout sliding along the surface of Ocean Avenue. I wondered if there were Indians in George Jessel's movie, but I decided he didn't seem the type who would be in a movie with Indians.

39

I BOARDED THE TRAIN at Union Station in Los Angeles on a gray morning. Larry had made sure the coffin containing my father's body had been loaded on the baggage car. He introduced me to the conductor who stood at the steps of the long green Pullman car that would be my home for the next three days. Next to me steam hissed from a pipe and great gobs of black grease oozed from the undercarriage. There was a throbbing from under the car just beyond us and the train seemed poised, as if it were tethered and only needed the shout from the conductor to release it on its journey.

Larry explained that I was accompanying my father's body to Kentucky where he was to be buried, that I was traveling alone, and that I would have to change trains in Chicago.

"Don't you worry, mister, we'll take good care of him." He pulled a gold watch from inside his uniform coat and looked at it, then down the platform toward the engine. I stood there, not knowing what to do until Larry put his arms around me and pulled me tight against him.

"You're going home in style, Tom Hall," he said. "And Eddie is going with you. He's not going in a tin can; he's going to ride in style. We were touched by luck. You and me and your father. It just came a little too late for him."

The conductor called out, "All aboard!" and we heard a short honk of the diesel engine.

"Don't you ever give up, Sport," he said. "He never did."

Neither of us cried. I felt again for the money belt that Larry had bought me, a thin black belt with a secret lining with twenty-five one-hundred-dollar bills neatly folded into it. I wore the belt underneath my trousers and I had promised him that I wouldn't take it off, no matter what. Then I climbed the steps into the vestibule, dragging my suitcase, the same one my father and I had with us when we left Chicago. It had only been eight months, but it seemed like a lifetime, and I felt far older. Dr. Metzenbaum's Captain had, as an afterthought, taken my childhood with him when he came for my father.

"Write to me!" Larry called out.

"I will. You, too!"

I wrestled open the heavy metal door. It had a pneumatic closer on it that made it hard to keep open and it took some time to wrestle the bag through it. There was a narrow corridor with an antiseptic-smelling men's room behind a dark curtain, and then the car opened up into rows of seats, two on each side, the seats facing each other in sets of four. The conductor was just behind me and he hoisted my bag into the rack overhead

"You need anything out of there, you just ask the porter," he said. "He'll be around in a bit." He pointed to a seat next to the window. Outside, Larry stood, his arms crossed over his chest, hugging himself. A woman ran by clutching her coat together with one hand, the other holding a newspaper over her head. It was beginning to rain. A man, bent nearly double, pulled a cart with hard rubber wheels piled high with trunks and boxes down the platform.

Larry waved and I waved and then we didn't know what to do. He called out something but it was only a movement of lips. The train jerked forward. Stopped. Jerked again. Slowly, imperceptibly, the platform began to move. Larry walked alongside the train that seemed not to move until he broke into a run and suddenly it was the train and not the platform moving. He slowed, stopped, turned away and was gone. I pressed my face tight to the glass in an effort to see him. I wished I had stayed at the open half door in the vestibule so that I could have leaned out the way people did in the movies, but it was too late. My father and I were on our way back to Chicago at last.

No one sat in the seats opposite me for the rest of the day. The porter came by, a small black man wearing a dark blue uniform and the same dark blue cap with a shiny black bill that the conductor wore. He told me he would make up the berths after supper and that he would make sure I had a seat in the dining car.

"They tell me we got your father on the train with us, too."

I nodded.

"We'll take good care of everything. I'll be with this car all the way to Chicago. You want anything, you'll find me there." He pointed forward to where I had passed the men's toilet. "I got me a little place in there. You needs anything at all—blankets, pillows, you want to know anything, you see me, hear?"

I nodded again. The southern California landscape slid by the window and by evening the orange groves and fields had turned barren and bleak. A man came through the car with what looked like a toy xylophone, playing three notes over and over, and I found out he was announcing that the dining car was open. Robert, the porter, came for me shortly after and pointed me down the train. I went through five cars, the vestibules roaring with wind and the clatter of banging metal and clacking wheels. The metal floor plates between the cars slipped back and forth and I could hardly keep my feet until I had pulled my way through the door into the next car.

The dining car was filled with the smell of roast chicken and coffee and had tables covered with gleaming white tablecloths, silver and china decorated with Indian designs. I had not known such things existed on trains. When my father and I came west, we ate sandwiches from a stash of bread and cheese and salami that we brought with us, and drank bottles of Dr. Pepper that he bought in the club car.

In the narrow corridor entering the dining car, I caught a glimpse through a partly opened door into a galley filled with steam and sweating black cooks in gleaming white coats and cook's hats, jammed into a tiny alley between stoves and ovens and racks of dishes and pans. I was seated opposite an older couple, a menu thrust into my hands by the dining car steward.

There was an array of dinners I didn't fully comprehend. But I knew immediately what fried chicken was and settled on that. It was dark outside and the black windows reflected only the dining car, leaving no sense of the train going anywhere except for the rhythmic clack of the wheels and the occasional light of a house in the distance wheeling slowly past.

The woman across from me asked if I was traveling by myself.

"No," I said. "I'm with my father."

"Isn't he coming to dinner?"

"He can't"

"Is he ill?" she persisted.

"Sort of," I said. "He's just not eating."

I didn't want to tell her that he was dead and in a box in the front of the train. Through the rest of the meal she pumped me for information and I told her we were coming back from visiting my uncle Larry, who was a famous horse trainer at Santa Anita race track, and that we lived in Kentucky which was where the Kentucky Derby was and that I went to a private school in Arizona called Metzenbaum Prep School for Boys. I was worried about how I would pay for the meal, but the waiter whispered that it was part of my ticket. Larry had thought of that, too.

I was glad to escape Mrs. Stein and her taciturn husband who nodded mostly at my stories as if he only half believed them. The Pullman car had been transformed in my absence. Gone were the seats. All that could be seen was a dimly lit corridor, the sides formed by the dark green curtains that covered the berths. The top berths had been pulled down from the ceiling by Robert and the facing seats had become the lower berth, a tiny rectangular room into which I crawled. Along the widow hung a net hammock for clothes and a little light next to the window gave off a yellow glow. Muffled sounds came from behind the curtains up and down the car as people got ready for the night. I lay, fully clothed, the shade up, light out, watching the darkness rush by. Once, during the night, I got up to go to the bathroom and found Robert dozing in a seat at the end of the men's room, waking when I pressed the handle to flush the toilet. At his feet were several pairs of men's shoes and a box with shoe shine polish and some rags.

"What you doing dressed at this hour of the night, boy?" he asked. "You get yourself back down there and get undressed and get yourself some sleep."

"Where do you sleep?" I asked.

"Right here. Three days I just cat naps. Plenty of time for Robert to sleep when we gets to Chicago. Now you go on, get out of here."

Back in the berth, I took off my shoes and trousers and pulled the covers up to my chin. I lay on my side, watching the landscape take shape as the light appeared. Once a train on a parallel track slammed past us with a great roar, the windows a blur only a few feet from mine, then gone in an absence of sound that left me breathless. Sagebrush gave way to trees; a river wound in a canyon below us and reappeared, the gray water turning green as dawn approached. A town went by, the platform racing past. I had the feeling that I was suspended above the earth and it was spinning beneath me.

Whispers broke the silence of the car, then muffled voices. When I looked out through the curtains I saw people in robes backing out of berths, men in their undershirts carrying shaving kits in the aisle. At the far end of the car Robert was folding back the curtains, the berths magically disappearing into the ceiling, luggage being stowed, seats reappearing. I put on my trousers and shoes and went to the men's room where I splashed cold water on my face, smoothed back my hair, listened to the men who talked with each other as easily as if they had known these strangers all their lives.

When I got back, my berth had become facing seats again. Some time early that morning we had crossed into Arizona and I had heard one of the men shaving at the row of metal bowls say that the next stop would be Flagstaff. I was afraid we had passed Williams, but we hadn't. This train, unlike the one my father and I had come west on, didn't stop at the smaller towns. The landscape became more familiar, the mountains turning blue in the distance, the tracks snaking through forests of pine and fir, then breaking out into the long open spaces that I remembered. Williams was a quick blur of brick buildings, the station marked by the clanging of the railway-crossing bell that came and went like a fire engine going by. There were several stopped cars, and the figures of people frozen on the street like the model people in the train layout at the Museum of Science and Industry in Chicago where I had spent Saturday mornings with my sister in some other life. Then we were in the open again. I could see the mountains where I knew Metzenbaum's people were lying facing the morning sun, and I pressed my face against the cool glass trying to see down the approaching tracks, waiting for Navajo Junction, but I was on the wrong side of the train; and when the three notes sounded for breakfast in the dining car, the train was slowing for Flagstaff.

There were patches of snow in the shade of buildings and the people on the platform puffed balloons of cold air. A cloud of steam enveloped the end of the car and we paused only long enough for a few people to board. I went to the end of the car and leaned out the open door, breathing the sharp air. Inside the car, the air had become stale, and I remembered the descriptive brochure from Dr. Metzenbaum's sanitarium, how the cold winter air of the Arizona mountains was a cure for almost anything. But it had not cured Mrs. Green or my father or Tiny. People died, no matter what kind of air they breathed, that much I now knew. Far down the train I saw the conductor lift his metal steps into a car, swing his hand up and down and disappear into the side of the train. There was a blast from the air horn on the snub-nosed diesel locomotive and we jerked ahead, picked up speed, and rumbled onward. The tracks curved and I could see the red-and-orange engine, painted as if it were an Indian headdress, the engineer's window glinting in the sun like a great bird's eye.

At dinner I shared the same table with Mr. and Mrs. Stein, but somehow she had ferreted out the news that I was traveling alone and that my father was dead and I was accompanying his casket on the train.

"I'm sorry to hear about your father," she said, not mentioning my stories about how rich he was or our plans to run a horse named The Chief in the Kentucky Derby. She reached across the table and patted my hand.

"You're a dear little thing," she said. "Was it an accident? He must have been a young man."

"It was tuberculosis," I said. "He had a hemorrhage and he coughed up all of his blood. It came out in bright pools and it covered everything. The nurses were soaked. You'd be surprised how much blood there is in a person's body."

Her face went white and she snatched back her hand as if she had touched a hot stove. Her husband's face went stiff.

"That wasn't necessary," he said.

"Yes it was." I knew he meant I shouldn't have been so graphic about the blood in front of his wife, but I could no longer hold back. I imagined the baggage car had racks of coffins—my father's and Mrs. Green's, the men from my father's cottage at Metzenbaum's, Tiny's—all presided over by a man who looked vaguely like a trolley car conductor, who wore a dark blue suit and a blue cap with a shiny black bill; but he had military ribbons on his chest and captain's bars on his shoulders, and he carried a motorman's wrench just like the drivers of the Red Cars in Los Angeles.

"Now he doesn't have any more blood," I said. "Just clear stuff that keeps him from spoiling until we get to Kentucky."

Mrs. Stein pushed her chair back from the table. "Come on, Henry," she said, reaching out for her husband.

"What the hell is wrong with you, kid?" he said, following her up the aisle.

"My father knew a man named Henry," I called out after him. "He was an Arctic explorer. They were together on the Russian Front." Heads turned at the other tables to see what was happening. I felt like crying, but I didn't want to in front of all those people.

After that I bought sandwiches in the club car and ate them at my seat by the window.

We crossed the Mississippi just past Fort Madison, Iowa, and then sped across the flatness that was Illinois, snow on all sides, the sky a muddy gray, towns coming often as we approached Chicago. The snow was dark with soot; bundled people stood frozen as we rushed past crowded brick houses.

Soon the tracks multiplied, black signal boxes stood in blackened snowdrifts and we entered the cavernous station echoing with the clatter of baggage carts, steam hissing in clouds around the waiting trains. The conductor reappeared to tell me that a woman from the railroad would come to the car for me and make sure I got on the train to Lexington. I thought maybe she would have a baggage cart with my father's casket, but when she appeared she told me the baggage had already been moved. We had an hour to wait and we spent it in the coffee shop where I had a hamburger and hot chocolate and a piece of pie and then we found the waiting train. It was evening again; she made sure the conductor knew who I was and that I was going to be met by my mother at Lexington. I never did ask her name.

Now the train was going south, plunging down the map as if gravity had hold of it, and I dozed in the seat, exhausted, filled with a lassitude that disconnected me from the rest of the restlessly sleeping people in the car. This was not a Pullman, only rows of seats with worn plush smelling of tobacco and wet wool, wax, and leather. Toward morning I began to see the landscape again, bare trees in squat clumps, forests that were a mixture of scrubby pine and oak, creeks with scarred banks that ran along the track, water the color of clay. Some of the trees had a pale green cast to them, the first buds of spring oozing out along the topmost limbs.

I expected the station at Lexington would be like the one in Los Angeles, a single building with a long platform so that I would be able to see my sister and my mother standing alone, waiting for me. I would step off the train, the man of the family now, the riches of the West in my slim black money belt; and my sister would run forward to embrace me, my mother hanging back. I think I was writing a novel in my head. Far down the platform my father's casket would be loaded into a high-wheeled baggage cart. I would learn to paint like Audubon. I would illustrate my own books. I would be famous. I wished my father could see it. The buds on the trees began to multiply until there was a brilliant green skimming the world.

CPSIA information can be obtained at www.ICGtesting.com
Printed in the USA
BVOW08s0254270315

393599BV00001B/2/P

9 780912 887258